"Remember, one false move and you'll be a soprano!"

Mattie scowled at him so he could read the message loud and clear.

"Hey, you offered to play the part," Ryan protested, but added a little too eagerly, "So when will you move in?"

"There's no use postponing bad medicine." Mattie shook her head disgustedly. "Tonight. But what I would like to know, Mr. Quinn, is why, all of a sudden, you're so willing to cooperate?"

"So, I'll tell you," Ryan muttered. "It's obvious that you don't like me. So, when this thing is over I won't have some woman hanging on my arm looking for something more. I reckon I have a better chance with you than with some simpleton who dreams fancy dreams."

"You're darn right," she threw back. "I can't imagine why any reasonable woman would want to marry you, Ryan Quinn!"

"Which you aren't. Reasonable, I mean."

Emma Goldrick describes herself as a
grandmother first and an author second. She was born
and raised in Puerto Rico where she met her husband,
a career military man from Massachusetts. His
postings took them all over the world, which often led
to mishaps—such as the Christmas they arrived in
Germany before their furniture. Emma uses the places
she's been as backgrounds for her books, but just in
case she runs short of settings, this prolific author and
her husband are always making new travel plans.

The Latimore Bride features the Latimore family first
introduced in *The Road* and *Tempered by Fire*.

Books by Emma Goldrick

HARLEQUIN ROMANCE

2739—THE TROUBLE WITH BRIDGES
2846—TEMPERED BY FIRE
2858—KING OF THE HILL
2889—TEMPORARY PARAGON
2943—TO TAME A TYCOON

HARLEQUIN PRESENTS

825—NIGHT BELLS BLOOMING
841—RENT-A-BRIDE LTD.
866—DAUGHTER OF THE SEA
890—THE OVER-MOUNTAIN MAN
953—HIDDEN TREASURES
1035—IF LOVE BE BLIND
1087—MY BROTHER'S KEEPER

The Latimore Bride

Emma Goldrick

Harlequin Books

TORONTO • NEW YORK • LONDON
AMSTERDAM • PARIS • SYDNEY • HAMBURG
STOCKHOLM • ATHENS • TOKYO • MILAN

Original hardcover edition published in 1988
by Mills & Boon Limited

ISBN 0-373-02967-5

Harlequin Romance first edition March 1989

CHAPTER ONE

MATHILDA LATIMORE pushed herself uneasily away from the edge of the rickety wooden dock at Omdurman and wished fervently that she hadn't come. A humid dry-season sun blazed down on her willowy frame and nipped at the edges of the strand of blonde hair that had escaped from under her pith helmet. It was close to the end of May, and the temperature at noon stood at thirty-eight degrees centigrade. Any minute now, any day, the Wet would be upon them. Tempers were high, tolerances low. Any little spark might set this world on fire.

Across the sullen waters, where the White Nile met the Blue, trapping the ancient capital of Khartoum in its V-shaped peninsula, she could see the prayer tower of the Two Niles Mosque, and catch a glimpse of its futuristic polygon geodesic dome. North of the junction, smoke hung lazily over the factory district of North Khartoum.

A cacophony of sound—in Arabic and the twenty-six Nilotic languages of the Democratic Republic of the Sudan—assailed her from all sides. The little paddle-wheel steamboat approaching the dock looked as if it might carry fifty passengers, and there were already more than three hundred standing waiting at the dock.

It serves me right, Mathilda told herself wryly. Where *is* that man? Everything that *could* go wrong, had. It had started off that way back in Boston, at the dinner table in the old house in Eastboro.

'The situation has gotten out of hand,' Bruce Latimore, her father, had said. 'That rail line was sup-

5

posed to be repaired three months ago. And we haven't heard one word from Quinn in the past thirty days. Somebody *has* to go.'

'It won't be you, Bruce,' his wife had interjected firmly. 'You're not over the 'flu yet. I didn't mean for you to get out of bed today, and I certainly am *not* going to let you hare off to Africa for some—railroad!' Mary-Kate Latimore was a tiny thing, but she spoke with authority, and as the matriarch of the Latimore clan, there were few—including her husband—who were prepared to go against her.

'We have a number of other supervising engineers,' Mathilda suggested.

'None who speak Arabic, Mattie,' her father reflected. 'And half of them too old for that sort of life. This is back-country. What we need is a young, dynamic engineer who speaks Arabic, and has no immediate assignments.'

'Well, don't look at me,' Mattie said hurriedly, that uneasy feeling creeping up her spine. 'I'm in the building business. I mean, I build buildings. I don't know a thing about railroads!' He *was* looking at her. Her mother was too.

'And I *studied* Arabic—I can't say that I speak it all that well,' she added, flustered.

'Nothing to worry about,' her father commented. 'We have a new man in Khartoum—Ryan Quinn. One of the best. And he speaks Arabic, and maybe half a dozen other languages besides.'

'Strange, I haven't met him before,' Mattie said defensively. 'I'm the vice-president of the corporation, and I haven't met a senior field man?'

'You were off in Mexico the last time he was here,' Mary-Kate said. 'You're always in too much of a hurry to go someplace else—do something more, Mattie.

Sometimes I wish you'd—well, it's not important! I liked him.'

'And that's all the recommendation I need?' laughed Mattie.

'And your father,' Mary-Kate interjected hurriedly. 'And don't forget that your sister Rebecca spent a year in Chad; that's right next door to the Sudan, so to speak.'

And that's something I'll do my best to forget, Mattie told herself. From Becky's description, it's not my favourite part of the world to which they're all trying to railroad me! She groaned at her own unintended pun.

'What's worrying you?' Bruce asked softly. 'You've been on plenty of overseas assignments with me.'

'Yes—well, that's the problem,' she sighed. '*With you*. Those are the key words. Now you want me out on my own, with some hard-hat who doesn't even know me? You both know what a struggle it is for a girl to gain any respect from construction men. Or do you mean to tell me this fellow Quinn is a pussycat?'

'Not exactly,' her mother said, agitated. 'In fact, I— I drew just the opposite conclusion. He seemed very——'

'Come on now, Mary-Kate,' Bruce chuckled indulgently. 'Mattie would be going out there as *my* representative. All she has to do is keep her cool, inspect everything, make headquarters-type noises, and then come home.'

'So you say,' his wife smiled up at him. With more than fondness, Mattie told herself. After all these years of marriage, they're still mad about each other!

'All right, out with it,' he demanded. His tiny wife shrugged her shoulders.

'It might be good for our Mattie,' she told them both. 'A part of her coming of age. But I vaguely remember that when one puts fresh meat in the tiger's cage, he sometimes eats.' Both Bruce and his daughter stared at the tiny judge, not understanding.

All of which had brought Mattie Latimore across half the world, her bags stuffed with anti-malaria pills, water purifiers, a *suitable* wardrobe, a very bad temper, and deposited her rather ungently in the middle of one of the world's trouble spots. Where in heaven's name was Mr Ryan Quinn?

'Ryan, I have a suspicion this is another wild-goose chase,' muttered Harry Crampton. The tall, husky man next to him pushed his lightweight bush hat back on his forehead, mopped the sweat off his forehead with a worn handkerchief, and shook his head in disgust.

'I believe it,' he muttered in return. 'See anything?'

'How can I tell?' grumbled Harry. 'What's he look like?'

'I haven't the faintest idea. Tall. Big, I suppose, like his old man. Mean. That father of his looked as if he wrestled black bears for sport and ate horseshoes. Blond, maybe. Hell, I don't know.'

'But why here, in Omdurman?'

'Because, dammit, he came in on the late-night flight six days ago, and registered at that fleabag in the centre of town. He's been to every government agency there is in the last six days, trying to get permits to move up-country, and I've always been a half-day behind him! The last office where I stopped told me that Matt Latimore had booked passage on the *Hurriya*. So there we are. Keep your damn eyes open, I've got enough troubles without losing the pro-consul of the Latimore empire!'

'Temper, temper, Ryan. Now look at that little lovely!' Harry Crampton, a beer-barrel of a man with a fifty-year-old fringe of white hair surrounding his bald head, had been up-country for a long time, and the peaches and cream blonde under the pith helmet was something to admire. A beige safari jacket clung to her slender figure—stuck to her, to be more exact, pasted on by her perspiration. The knee-length matching skirt might have been stylish in Boston; here it clung to the fullness of her buttocks in a manner that would make any man just the slightest bit hungry.

'Hell, I don't have time for that,' Ryan Quinn growled. 'Why the people back in Boston think I need a nursemaid I'll never know! I don't have time for this horsing around. I've already spent a month in the back country without success.'

His companion grunted sympathy, but the little steamcraft had already tied up, and the gangplank, two three-foot-wide boards, was shoved ashore. The crowd milled and then rushed. Four Masakin Tiwal, willowy black crew members who towered above six foot eight, and were dressed in tribal scars and loincloths, swung over the side of the boat to maintain some sort of order.

Passengers flocked aboard. About half were dressed in European clothing—long-sleeved shirts, long cotton trousers. Another quarter wore Arabic dress, an *aba* covered by the traditional cloak-like *djellaba*, or more simply, a white *gallabiya*, that might best be described as a long plain nightshirt. Turbans proliferated, but a few reminders of desert nobility could be seen, wearing the white headcloth fastened with the rope-like, multi-coloured *kafiyeh*. And, as to be expected in a multi-racial nation, a few Dinka refugees were aboard, their ash-polished black skins sparkling in the sunlight, wearing as little as possible in deference to the Moslem laws.

'Wait till the last,' said Ryan Quinn. 'If he doesn't show, we'll have to get back. There's bound to be hell to pay by now, anyway!'

'Looks like our little lady means to go along,' Harry chuckled. 'Why do you suppose someone like that would ride the river?'

'Maybe because she can't afford the train or the bus,' Ryan Quinn snarled. 'Don't, for God's sake, start off with that "helping hand" routine—she's young enough to be your daughter!'

'Maybe,' Harry grinned. 'But *you're* only thirty-five. Just right!' He touched the brim of his bush hat sarcastically, and walked over to the girl.

Mattie watched him come. Practically all the other passengers had gone aboard and crowded on to the open deck that stretched forward from the wheelhouse to the bow. A few had gone aft, where the deck was sheltered by a brightly coloured awning. Her mind was a little bewildered, compounded by an uneasy stomach and six nights with little sleep.

'You sure you're on the right dock?' Harry Crampton asked, removing his hat. The Middle-West twang marked him at once as an American, and she sighed in relief.

'I don't know,' she confessed. Her soft contralto, modified by her New England accent, was just enough to charm him. And besides, she told herself, he looks like Uncle Charlie! How could I go wrong with him? Now if it were that other guy over there—look at the frown on his face! Mean! I'll bet he eats horseshoes for lunch! 'They told me at the travel office that I could get to Kosti by boat. This one was the first departure. My arrangements have—fallen through.' And I'll beat up Ryan Quinn when I find him! Up one side and down the other, she thought fiercely. 'So I decided to go ahead by myself.'

'Bad country for a woman travelling alone,' Harry said mildly. 'You should have taken the train. Here, let me help you with your gear.' He shouldered one of her three suitcases and took another in his hand. 'This is all you brought?' he asked cautiously.

'All I brought?' She gave him one of her patented Latimore smiles—the ones her father swore could be used to wind clocks back in Massachusetts. 'I thought I was bringing too much!' She picked up her third suitcase with both hands and straggled after him up the gangplank. He turned left, towards the stern. A surprised Moslem officer at the head of the gangplank stared at her, then made a check-mark on his passenger list.

'It's not a matter of quantity as much as it's a matter of quality,' Harry tossed over his shoulder, leading her back into the shade. The whistle up on the bridge sputtered, spurted, and managed a reasonably accurate 'toot'. Mattie could feel the deck shifting under her feet. There was neither cabin nor chair to be seen. Harry dropped her bags in the well of the stern.

'Best place to be,' he commented. 'You get the breeze all the time, and people don't fall over you. Stake this place out.'

'But I asked for first-class passage,' she said firmly. 'I thought——'

'This is it,' chuckled Harry. 'First-class in the stern, second-class in the bow—shade. Running water over there—but don't drink it.'

'That's it?'

'That's it. By the way, my name is Crampton. Harry Crampton.'

They stood at the stern rail, watching the paddle wheels stir up the muddy water. The White Nile was not exactly white. As, for that matter, the Blue Nile was not exactly blue. The river looked angry and dirty—moving slowly north towards Egypt. The big man, probably Harry's compatriot, came to join them, and Mattie looked at him out of the corner of her eyes. Just the sort of man you'd love to hate, she thought. Six feet two, perhaps. Brown hair, brown eyes, a square face fixed in gloom. Broad, square shoulders and a thick neck—just what you would expect of a typical football player! Big, dumb, strong and arrogant. She rolled the phrases over on her tongue, enjoying them.

'Crampton—Harry Crampton,' the older man repeated, holding out his hand. 'Construction. On our way to Kosti.'

'Latimore,' she returned with a smile, dropping her long, slender hand into his paw. 'Mattie Latimore. I'm in construction, too.'

'Oh——!' the big stranger next to Harry muttered, using an old four-letter word from the barnyard. He glared at her, his face turned from sun-tanned brown to choking red, then he wheeled around and marched angrily away.

'You have to understand,' Harry told Mattie as they sat on the deck against the rail some hours later. 'He has a lot on his mind. There's all kinds of trouble about the railroad, he doesn't care for headquarters snoopers, and he has considerable trouble relating to the fact that you——' he stumbled over a couple of consonants and stopped talking.

'That I'm a woman, I suppose?' She shook her head in disgust. In this day and age? Of course, she knew chauvinism existed everywhere, especially in Boston. And in a tough trade like construction it was hard for a woman to make her mark. Half her good luck might well be due to her brain and her honours degree from the Massachusetts Institute of Technology, but the other half, she readily admitted, came from being Bruce Latimore's daughter. 'Well, I can't help that,' she sighed. 'He'll either have to get used to it, or——'

'Or what?' The man under discussion had sauntered up behind them. His deep voice was soft but penetrating; not exactly something to help her admire him. Had he sported a weak tenor, or some other deficiency, she would have felt better. Still, a good supervisor goes out of her way to get along with the help! She turned and looked up, smiling.

'Or the sky will fall, Chicken Little,' she teased.

Ryan was in no mood for compromise. All he could see in the twilight was the slimness of her as the wind took her shoulder-length straight hair, the gleam in her blue eyes, the slight swell of her pert breasts. And *she* was sent to spy on *me*! For two cents I'd turn in my resignation, he thought bitterly. There are a million things left undone, and I don't have the patience to nursemaid a headquarters type.

'You expect to be here long?' he enquired.

'You sound eager to help me go back home,' she said, with a touch of anger in her voice. 'I wish you could have been as eager to help me arrive. I'll be here as long as it takes.'

'Hey, it's not my fault,' he grumbled. 'It's a hundred and sixty miles from Kosti to Khartoum. I ran into a government road block, and they delayed us.'

'For six days?' she asked incredulously.

'For six days and some hours,' Harry added mournfully. 'We didn't have the right government stamp on our travel papers.'

'So all the time I've been sweating it out, pushing around Khartoum like some fool, getting signatures from every official ever appointed, you've been sitting in some hotel, taking things easy!' Mattie's voice broke in anger. What I'd like to do, she told herself angrily, is punch him in the mouth. But I'm afraid he'd hit me back!

'Yes, of course,' said Ryan Quinn, boredom riding every word.

'Hey, it wasn't exactly like that,' Harry protested. 'We spent all that time in the jail at Sennar—and then required another day getting ourselves deloused!'

Mattie squirmed around to look directly at Ryan Quinn. 'You could have mentioned that,' she said quietly. 'I'm not exactly a dunce. I would have understood.'

'Would you?' he snapped. 'If you were, you'd be the first woman I ever met who understood *anything*!'

'Hooey!' she snorted. 'Have I fallen in with the only misogynist in Africa?'

'I don't think so,' Harry interrupted unhappily. 'If that means what I think it does, there are one or two more. Possibly three. Wait until you meet Artafi.'

She looked at him, mystified.

'He's the reason why the railroad doesn't work,' Harry hastened to add. 'Tell you all about it in Kosti—if we get there. Time for a little chow-down, lady.'

'Sounds good to me,' Mattie agreed. 'Where's the kitchen?'

'Kitchen?' Both men spoke at the same time.

'Don't tell me,' groaned Ryan. 'You didn't bring any food?'

'Of course I didn't bring any food,' Mattie returned angrily. 'I told you, I bought a first-class ticket. When do they serve the meal?'

'Oh, God help me,' Ryan moaned, rubbing his hands against his forehead. 'Look, Little Miss Innocence, this isn't the Mississippi River we're on. Your first-class ticket gets you a ride under an awning. It ought to take about—oh—forty-eight hours. They don't serve food—you have to bring it with you. Hell, if they *did* serve, you'd be crazy to eat it. American stomachs aren't ready for

African bugs, no more than Africans are ready for American bugs.'

'OK,' she sighed, 'so I'll go hungry for a couple of days. At least I'll have some water to drink.'

'And thank God for that,' he snarled. 'Who reminded you to bring your own water?'

'Bring?' she said weakly. 'I should have—nobody reminded me!' Somebody should have, she raged to herself. You, Ryan Quinn, when you met me at the plane, the way you were supposed to! You're the one responsible. When you were supposed to be reminding me about all this stuff, you were sitting comfortably in a jail, scratching—oh, brother, I can't blame him. Scratching. Brush it off. 'Dear lord, you make this sound like Darkest Africa!'

'It is,' he snapped, enjoying her confusion.

'But—there's a faucet over there. The ship has water!'

'Of course they do,' he replied gently. 'We're in a freshwater river. They pump it up out of the Nile. Why don't you help yourself? By tomorrow you'll be enjoying Pharaoh's Revenge!'

Mattie took one quick look over the side. The river was no longer the garbage disposal trench it was around Khartoum, but even here, out in the countryside, it looked hardly potable. On the other hand, Becky had told her all about African water. All she had to do was fill a cup with—fill a cup? 'I—don't suppose I could borrow a cup anywhere?' she asked hesitantly.

'Just happen to have one with me,' Harry allowed. He had been sitting back, a little grin playing at the corners of his mouth, as he watched the battle. Now he fished in his backpack and pulled out a battered tin cup— larger than a teacup, not quite as big as a coffee mug. His smile grew broader as he looked over her head at Ryan Quinn's glare. 'Might happen to have one or two extra sandwiches,' he continued mildly. 'What you plan to do with the cup?'

'Drink,' said Mattie determinedly. She swayed gracefully up to her feet and took the proffered cup.

'Hey, I don't want to have to send your father condolences,' Ryan called after her as she walked unsteadily over towards the tap clamped on the corner of the pilothouse. 'It's on your own head!'

'You'd better believe it,' she muttered as she filled the cup, dropped in two purification tablets, and sauntered back, trying not to spill a drop. The tablets sizzled and dissolved; the water sat, the sediment settled to the bottom of the cup. Fifteen minutes, Becky had said. Her thirst was increasing by the minute, watching.

'Lost your nerve?' taunted Ryan. 'Struck by common sense?'

'You bet,' she said quietly, and slugged the contents of the cup down without disturbing the sediment.

'Crazy,' he muttered. 'Pure, unadulterated crazy! I might as well start composing that letter to your father.'

'You do that,' she said sweetly, and turned her back on him.

'Put something in that, did you?' Harry asked softly.

'Believe I did,' she chuckled. 'I have a sister—well, to tell the truth, I have three sisters and a brother. But this particular sister is a doctor who served her internship in Chad. And her husband is a doctor who was chief of surgery for the Army. They gave me some magic pills. I don't know what's in them, but two tablets in a glass of swamp water kills everything that moves, lives, swims, or even *thinks* about making trouble.'

'Damn you!' snarled Ryan Quinn as he got up and walked away, pounding one fist into the palm of his other hand.

'I do believe you've got his number,' laughed Harry. 'How about a—well, don't ask what kind—how about a sandwich? Guaranteed not to grow penicillin. Maybe I should qualify that. The guarantee ran out five days ago. Got another pill?'

'No,' she smiled, 'but I've got a cast-iron stomach. If you'll eat one, I will.'

The two of them settled back against the rail and enjoyed. As is usual in countries near the Equator, the twilight was short; black night fell swiftly. The Nile was at low water, sunk down far below its banks, waiting for the rains to come. First the local rains, and then for months the rains on the Equatorial mountains, all draining into the river system. They were moving through the Sudanese plain. Farmers and cattle herdsmen had moved close to the river for water. As the Nile rose they would move farther away, dispersing against the floods. As a result there were little open fires in every corner as the riverbed twisted and turned gently, and the proud little *Hurriya* paddled on her way.

'The stars look so close,' murmured Mattie as, her sandwich finished, she leaned back to look out over the stern. 'Is there a moon?'

'Comes along right on schedule,' Harry informed her. 'But for that you need a younger man than me.'

'Not true,' Mattie said stoutly. 'I can take 'em or leave them alone, and right at the moment I'm in a "leave them alone" phase. What is the *matter* with that man?'

'Hard to tell. He's a man in a hurry. I've known him for a while. He's been out here for six or seven years, working for different companies. Divorced. Must have been one hell of a bust-up—the only mail he gets is from her lawyers.'

'Well, that's no skin off *my* nose,' she offered. 'I don't think I've ever met a man less likely to be liked than him!'

'Somehow,' Harry laughed, 'I get the impression that you two might be cut out of the same cloth.'

Mattie raised her eyebrows. 'Yes, I've heard it said by one or two others that that's true. Not that I'm admitting it, mind you. Who told you that?'

'Nobody told me,' he said. 'I just call them like I see them. Had enough to eat?'

'Plenty,' she answered, 'but I'm dying for a bath. You don't suppose I could just—slip over the side, maybe? We aren't going too fast, and if you'd promise to look the other way?'

'Wouldn't be any trouble not to look,' he said solemnly, 'but I don't recommend it—unless you've got one of those pills big enough to purify the whole river?'

'Now what?' she grumbled. 'Piranha, or some man-eating crocodile?'

'Might be a crocodile or two,' he reflected, 'although they prefer slow water. No, the problem with the Nile, even this far south, is bilharzia.'

'Bila who?'

'Bilharzia,' he repeated. 'Liver flukes. A lovely little thing that chews its way into your innards, and just won't come out. Blindness is *the* major tropical disease in Egypt, the Sudan, and Uganda. We have showers at our place in Kosti, and I'd recommend you hold off until then. Lord, I'm tired! It's been a tough day.'

'I—forgot to ask about that,' Mattie said. 'Beds? Hammocks?'

'Not on this little stretch of river,' he laughed. 'There's not much call for that sort of service. Why didn't you take the railroad or the bus?'

Ryan Quinn came back, looming up out of the sunset. Big ears, Mattie told herself, listening all the time and trying to hide the fact. Well, let him snoop!

'I couldn't.' She shifted her weight to get more comfortable. 'At the tourist bureau they showed me the map. The road and the railroad go up the Blue Nile, not the White. And then you have to change at some place called—Sennar, I think it was, before you cross the hills to Kosti. On the other hand, the map shows the river runs almost straight. They told me I could go up the river——'

'Just a minute,' Ryan interrupted. 'They spoke English?'

'Not exactly,' she laughed, remembering the scene in that crowded little office. 'They—well, it was sort of a combination between my terrible Arabic and their terrible English.'

'And they told you you could ride the river from Khartoum to Kosti?' he persisted. Mattie was becoming annoyed.

'Of course,' she snapped, then thought back. 'Well— perhaps not exactly. I said something like—is it possible to go up the river from here to Kosti? And they said *yes*.'

Ryan grinned down at her. Even Harry laughed.

'What's that mean?' she asked cautiously.

'Oh, it means that they didn't exactly lie,' chuckled Ryan. 'You might as well settle down. You'll see.'

'I'll see what?' she shouted after him as he walked away again. 'I'm tired of looking at his back,' she muttered to herself. 'I've only known him a couple of hours, and that's three too many!'

'I have a blanket,' Harry offered. 'It gets a little cold on the river at night. Not that the temperature gets terribly low, but the contrast between night and day is pretty severe. Want it?'

'Lord, no,' she sighed. 'I wouldn't want to take your only blanket. Besides, Mr Wonderful is coming back over here. I'm sure he'll provide enough warmth for all of us.'

Harry grunted a non-reply, wrapped himself up in his blanket, and stretched out on the steel deck. Ryan Quinn came over beside her in the dark, fumbled in his pack, and unrolled a bedroll. He seemed to be talking to himself as he worked—it couldn't just be indigestion, Mattie told herself. And it was getting cool. She hunched up, pulling her knees up into her stomach and wrapping her arms around them for warmth.

Ryan Quinn worked easily in the darkness, like a man whose every movement was pre-planned. Graceful, Mattie thought, I'll give him that. He moves well. But then, so do lions, and I understand they have terribly bad breath!

'Is this how you plan to spend the night?' he asked. The noises around them were dying down. Conversations on the forward deck had faded into nothing. A tiny baby cried and was comforted. The paddle-wheels whapped at the water in a slow rhythm that was almost hypnotising. There was a heavy smell of manure wafting off the land, ploughed and waiting for the first rains and planting.

'I—guess so,' she replied. 'Choices seem somewhat limited.'

'They do, don't they?' It was the first agreeable statement she had heard him make. As if the darkness hides him, and so he can afford to be friendly, she thought. And isn't that a funny thing to think? They didn't teach psychology at MIT—not in *her* major.

'Yes,' she half whispered, trying not to waken Harry.

'Don't worry about him,' said Ryan. 'A herd of charging elephants couldn't wake him up once he's dropped off.'

'That's what it is,' she commented. 'I *knew* something was wrong somewhere. It should have been "a herd of buffalo" wouldn't wake him up. It's the foreignness of it all that I'm hearing!'

'I haven't the faintest idea what you're talking about,' he returned, shaking his head and moving closer. 'Is there something wrong with my ears? You hear foreignness?'

'Don't struggle with it,' she laughed. Her voice ran gently down-scale like a waterfall. 'I made up the word—and the idea. I remember—about two years ago, Dad and I were drifting down the Amazon in a canoe. I was *much* younger then——'

Ryan waited for a moment, but no words followed. 'Yes, of course.' His words were solemn, but rimmed in laughter—friendly laughter. Or so it seemed.

What kind of man is he, really? her conscience queried. Friendly laughter? Don't kid yourself! If he barks like a dog, smells like a dog, bites like a dog—chances are he is a dog! Right?

'Look,' Ryan broke in on her reverie, 'it's going to get a lot colder before dawn. I've a double bedroll here. Why don't you climb in? We don't have to like each other to keep ourselves warm.'

'No, thank you,' Mattie said very distantly, very coolly. 'My mother didn't raise any idiot daughters.'

'Are you sure?'

'I'm sure.' There was enough finality in her tone to turn off the House of Representatives, but it washed over him with practically no effect.

'Well, don't say I didn't offer,' he rejoined. 'If you change your mind, just remember I hate to go to bed with a woman who won't take off her boots.'

'You should be so lucky,' she snapped, and turned her back on him. The moon *was* coming up. Low and yellow on the horizon, it balanced on the far peaks of Ethiopia, then sprang into the middle of the heavens, convoyed by the evening star.

'How many Pharaohs have seen this, just like this?' she muttered to herself. 'Downstream a good way, I know, but still sharing the Nile, the Mother of Life. How many?' Two shapes, geese, flew across the face of the moon, sending a little chill down her back. She huddled back into her corner, counting the movements of the walking beam that turned the paddle-wheels. The wheels turned, the water churned, but the boat seemed to remain still. It was the land on either side that was moving, un-rolling in a great panorama painted by an artist thousands of years gone. She shuddered.

'For God's sakes, your teeth are chattering enough to keep us all awake,' growled Ryan, close beside her.

'You didn't have to come here,' she snapped, close to tears. 'There's plenty of space over on the port side.' He grunted and turned over. She glared at him in the moonlight. There he was, all snug and warm, with nothing to do but make snide remarks! Mattie stabbed at her tears with a knuckle. When I get back to Boston, she promised, I'm going to have him fired. Or worse, I'll send him to our office in Cleveland! Why am I crying? Homesick, at my age? I've been away from home a hundred times. Not that it wouldn't be wonderful having Mary-Kate here. And isn't that stupid! A girl needs her father at a time like this, not her mother. But Mary-Kate is so easy to talk to—so—sensible! What would Ma do in a situation like this?

Her whole body shook with the shivers that ran up and down her spine, and a voice whispered in her ear from miles away. Get in the sleeping-bag, stupid. What can he do to you on an open deck in the middle of three hundred people? It might not have been her stepmother's voice—but then again, maybe it was. Mary-Kate Latimore was descended from a long line of Salem witches.

Warily, her mind made up, Mattie sidled across the deck and laid back the top of the double sleeping-bag. Ryan was huddled in one corner, completely out of the way. She slipped her feet into the warmth, then pulled them out again. 'I hate to go to bed with a woman who won't take off her boots!' She tugged at the laces and pulled both her ankle-high heavy boots off, tying the laces of one to the laces of the other. At least she knew *that* much about camping in the tropics. One shoe isn't worth a nickel. Better to lose two at the same time; two made it a little harder for light fingers to help you out.

There was a small hood at the top of the bag. She slipped her shoes and socks into its cavity, and followed suit, sliding her slender length down deeper and deeper in the warmth. Ryan stirred and she froze, holding her breath. In another moment he turned back on his side. She resumed her slow movement, savouring the warmth, the kapok softness between her bones and the steel deck.

All the hustle and bustle of life—the air travel, the excitement, the panic on arrival, the frustration of dealing with bureaucracy, the confusions of meetings—all conspired to close her eyes and send her off. She completely missed the fact that Ryan was lying there, brown eyes caressing her golden hair, silvered by the moon, grinning at her. So deep was her sleep that she hardly noticed a thing when he coiled up next to her back, spoon fashion, and one of his big hands came across her side and clutched gently at the softness of her breast. It *did* lead her to some exciting, erotic dreams—

of a type seldom stimulated in her by the men she knew. And never in this mad, wild fashion.

She came drowsily half awake some time in the middle of the night when the paddle-wheels came to a temporary stop. Her fashionable safari jacket was all unbuttoned, and his hand was in full occupation of her unfettered breast. For a second she panicked, but only for a second. It was—comforting. For a moment, she told herself. Only for a moment. But the moment ran on into time, and she fell asleep, leaving him in sole possession of the battlefield.

CHAPTER TWO

IT WAS the music that woke her. Mattie pried one eye open to check on conditions. Waking up was never her favourite sport. Somewhere out of sight on the forward deck, a couple of somebodies were beating on little tambour drums, while a reed pipe keened an atonal song. There was dancing, too. She could hear the slap of bare feet on steel, and occasionally a dancer or player would shout a phrase or two, which would be followed by laughter from all sides.

Mattie managed to prop herself up with both arms, and looked around carefully. Her neck was stiff, but then so was her back, her thighs, her upper legs. The other side of the bedroll was empty. A second of panic fled as she remembered. A quick move of her hand showed that her safari jacket was buttoned to the top—something she would never have done. And then there was the smell of hot coffee.

'Need to be rescued?' She turned her head slowly to keep it from falling off. Ryan Quinn was kneeling beside her, a mug in his hand, from which a spiral of steam arose. Hot black coffee. She pulled herself up and seized the mug with both hands. Its warmth was a blessing. In the pre-dawn darkness, the wind from the river had dropped off. Or was it something else?

Mattie could smell the river. The air was full of scents, but mostly it was earth that tantalised her nostrils, good strong turned earth, with the springtime smell it carried, overladen with odour of dung, liberally used. All that information registered, but the most important fact did

25

not—not until she looked around her and realised. The paddle-wheels had stopped!

'Where—where are we?' she muttered as she sipped at the coffee.

'El Geteina,' Ryan told her. The name meant nothing to her, but she had no intention of admitting it. She gulped at the drink, and almost burned her tongue.

'So why did we stop?'

'It would be pretty hard to go much farther upstream.' She stared up, barely able to make out his face in the poor light. There's something about this, she told herself cautiously, that smacks of 'and here's where the stupid little girl gets hers!'

'And that makes you so happy?'

'You bet it does,' he returned. 'Drink up, lady. We have to get off here.'

'But I bought a ticket to Kosti!' Mattie had finished off the coffee, and struggled out of the sleeping-bag. Ryan gestured casually upstream. She wandered over to the rail, her eyes still sleep-laden, and looked. Directly ahead, no more than half a mile away, the curved back of a huge dam-site blocked the passage. On the far side, a spume of water shot out from the base of the dam. 'What——?' she began.

'The White Nile dam,' he told her caustically.

'But they told me at the tourist office that——'

'You mean *you* told *them*!' he muttered. 'Typical American! You didn't ask, you told.' He shifted into a mocking falsetto. 'Oh, yes, it is *possible* to go by steamer from Khartoum to Kosti. Isn't that what they told you?'

Never one to hide behind her mistakes, Mattie nodded grimly. 'They lied to me.'

'Oh, no, they didn't,' he chuckled. 'They told you the absolute truth. It is *possible*! But there's a four-mile gap in the trip. Come on. The trucks are waiting to haul us around the dam, and another steamer is waiting on the other side.'

It was a mistake. She marked it down in her memory. A Latimore trait, that, to learn from your mistakes. Only she resented the fact that she had had to learn it from this great bear of a man, this thoroughly objectionable—person! Angrily she shook herself free from his hand, picked up her scattered luggage, and stalked over towards the port-side gangplank.

'Don't be in such a damn hurry,' Ryan told her as he caught up. He snatched her bags out of her hands, handling them as if they were featherweight material. 'Watch your step.'

'Thank you,' she said with as little grace as she could manage. He was still chuckling as he followed her down the gangplank and over to the waiting truck. And *that* was something else she marked down in her memory for future use!

The *Falashi* might easily have been the *Hurriya*, transported by some magic over the towering dam. Up on the forward deck little charcoal braziers were lit, sending their pungent smoke straight back as the paddle-wheels drove the ship south.

'I stopped long enough to buy us some supplies,' Harry told them as they clustered around their own little brazier. 'I'll have more coffee in a minute, and then we'd better get back to sleep. It's a long haul to Kosti.'

Mattie tendered him a warm smile, then walked over to the rail, her arms wrapped around herself for warmth. Behind them she could see the towering dam. Around her the horizon had disappeared as they steamed down the middle of the huge man-made lake. Gulls were diving in their wake, fishing for the garbage thrown over the side. The sun, still not yet above the horizon, heralded its coming with a tiny rim of light, and a promise of more heat to come. She was locked up inside her own mind when Ryan came over to stand beside her.

'Coffee's ready,' he announced. 'And if it makes you feel better, I'm sorry.'

'About what?' she queried, matching a puzzled expression to her question. So I remember everything, she told herself, but I'm darn well not going to let him know it. Maybe a few pangs of conscience would be good for his soul!

'Oh,' he muttered. Silence for a moment. 'Well, when you climbed into my——'

'The only limitation you set was that I take my boots off,' she interrupted. 'I did. I hope I didn't disturb you?'

'Disturb? Oh—no, of course not.'

Mattie hunched herself back until she was leaning on the rail, and sipped at the fresh, savoury brew. *Falashi* was not exactly hurrying. There was a wind blowing across the river, creating little waves that crashed into the ship's wake and were instantly absorbed. The flock of gulls followed along behind them, like the tail of a kite.

Ryan was squatting on his heels beside her, nursing his own mug. That craggy face had still not relaxed. He looked about as friendly as Pharaoh Rameses, sitting in his huge monumental niche far downstream. Mattie fished for some conversation. 'Where are we now?' she asked.

'Kordofan.' He gave a weak gesture with his right hand. 'We're about halfway to Kosti, making good time. We should pull in there by nine or ten o'clock tonight.'

'Kordofan? Isn't that the area of that terrible famine a year ago?'

'One of them,' he grunted. 'At the end of the drought, there was hardly a blade of grass growing between here and the mountains.'

'And now?'

'Oh, they had a good year this last year. There's plenty of food in the Sudan, and plenty of people still starving. The government can't make the distribution programme work. The port is full of ships, the ships are crammed with food, and the people are hungry.'

'Well, that's why we contracted to rebuild the railroad,' Mattie snapped. 'If it had been done on time——'

'You need to look at your contracts more closely,' he said roughly. 'Repair and operate the railroad—that's what it says. The repair's been done, long since. Are you some sort of railroad engineer?'

'Not—exactly,' Mattie muttered, fishing around behind her for her boots. He did show a little gleam of approval as she very carefully turned the boots upside-down, one at a time, and thumped them to force out any wandering visitors before putting her feet inside. But it was the tiniest of smiles, and he smothered it as soon as he saw her looking.

Might as well take the bull by the horns, she told herself. 'You don't like me, Mr Quinn.' Not a question; a flat statement.

'Is there some requirement that I like you?' he asked distantly. 'I don't remember anything like that in my contract.'

'Would you mind telling me why?'

'Yes.'

'Yes what?'

'Yes, I would mind telling you.' He terminated the conversation by rising gracefully to his feet and walking away. Mattie struggled, one foot booted, the other not, then decided it wasn't worth the effort. She gulped the coffee down, went back to the bedroll, and promptly went back to sleep.

The next time she woke up it was late afternoon, and Harry Crampton was beside her. 'Doing guard duty,' the older man explained. 'Looked as if you didn't plan to wake up at all.'

'Couldn't see any reason to,' she grumbled. 'Why do I need to be guarded?'

'You're in a land where the average income is just over three hundred and forty dollars a year,' he told her. 'Doesn't take much to lead people into thievery.'

'Which is our responsibility as much as the thief's,' added Ryan Quinn, from her other side, in a booming bass voice that made her fragile head wince.

'Don't start that, Ryan,' said Harry. 'Mattie here didn't invent the system.'

'Perhaps not,' the other man returned, 'but running around flaunting gold rings, fancy purses, Neiman-Marcus clothes, when people around them haven't a pit to hiss in, well——'

'Pit to hiss in?' she mused. 'I've heard that before in a less sanitised version. You're actually making a joke, Mr Quinn! It would be *so* much better if you would give us a hint when you do that. Maybe a little smirk, a lift of the lip—something like that?'

'God,' he muttered, 'why me? First they send me a supervisor that I don't need, then it turns out she's female, and on top of all *that* misery she's a humourist! Why me, God?'

'Punishment for your past indiscretions,' she returned solemnly. 'Either in your present or some past life. I see you as a great reincarnation, Mr Quinn. Simon Legree? The Marquis de Sade? Dracula? Something along those lines. But you don't *look* like a man who hates women!' She opened her eyes wide and stared up at him, and gave him an example of one of her grade-

A smiles. It bounced off him as if he were wearing armour plate. 'And besides, I wasn't *flaunting* anything!'

'I don't hate *real* women, Miss Latimore,' he said in a silky-smooth voice. 'There's a place for *real* women in my life.'

'That's interesting,' she snapped. 'In your bed, I suppose?'

'Oh, that and other places. But you hardly qualify, *Mattie.*'

He pronounced the name in such a fashion that it was an insult all by itself. As if he were saying, 'Go out and play on the highway with your dolls, you little monster!' Enough steam was being generated in *her* boilers to drive the *Falashi* at twice its present speed.

'So why don't I qualify?' she threw at him, her blue eyes sparking fire and damnation.

'I—two reasons,' he stated flatly. 'First, I like my women to be more—robust.'

'So I'll practise deep breathing,' she retorted, doing just that. The result was not too impressive, even to her angry eyes.

'And second, I like my women to wait until they're asked,' Ryan said placidly.

'*Your women!*' Mattie echoed as she exhaled with a gusty sigh. And then, deep in her mind, she could hear Mary-Kate. The first person to lose her temper in an argument has lost the game, her mother always said. Keep cool. Dig around the edges. *Argumentum ad hominem* never makes it!

She forced a bright smile on to her face. 'Well, it's going to be an interesting few weeks, Mr Quinn. You will remember, of course, that I'm the vice-president of the company, and that you work for me?'

Ryan Quinn glared down at her and shook his head. 'Women!' he muttered. And then, louder, 'My contract has only a few weeks to go, lady. It's probably luck for both of us!'

There were a thousand things she wanted to say to him, none of them too polite, but he closed off the opportunity by stalking away from her, leaving her fuming.

'You and the boss don't seem to get along all that well,' said Harry Crampton as he came over. 'Try some of this for breakfast.'

'We don't, do we?' she sighed. 'Somehow or another he riles me. He doesn't have to say anything; just standing still he gets my goat! What is this stuff?' The question came after her second bite. She was too hungry to wait for an answer.

'It's called way-bread,' he answered. 'Unleavened bread, baked especially for travel, to be eaten "on the way", so to speak. You can stuff it with meats and sauces and things if you're so inclined. I put olive oil on it—that's the local custom.'

'Tastes good,' she mumbled around a mouthful. 'Hell, anything would taste good, even a bite of roast Quinn!' The startled look on his face brought her back to earth. Whatever else he was, Harry Crampton was a loyal worker. Loyal to Ryan Quinn, that was.

'I didn't mean I'm a practising cannibal,' she chuckled. 'Besides, he'd be way too tough for my teeth.'

'I'm glad you recognise that,' Harry said solemnly. 'And cannibal jokes aren't too popular around these parts, either!'

'That's just a sample of the Latimore family disease,' Mattie said soberly. 'How long have you known our Mr Quinn?'

'I don't exactly remember. This is the third job I've been on with him in Africa. He's a good boss, but hates to take orders. Well known in Africa, he is. Must be a dozen countries that know Ryan Quinn. Good-looking boy, too.'

'If you like that kind,' Mattie muttered indignantly, digging into the bread.

The afternoon passed quickly. Gradually the boundaries of the great lake appeared, and finally they were on the river again. The riverbanks were lower than before, or perhaps the water level was higher. 'By the middle of next month, after the rains come, the river will start rising,' Harry explained. 'By the end of August it will be up a good twenty feet over what you can see here. They won't need the *sagia* then.' He pointed to where a series of waterwheels, driven by oxen, were lifting water from the river up to the fields.

The country was changing from the sandy littoral of the north to grass plains, brown in the sun of the Dry. Palm trees clustered along the banks, with tamarind and acacia growing behind them. Clusters of little round huts with steeply thatched conical roofs replaced the walled villas of the north. Vast cotton fields, newly ploughed, stretched to the horizon as the farmers waited for the first rains before they planted the year's second crop. The people were different, too. Skins were darker. The turban had disappeared, although the *djellaba* was still worn. And women had come out from under the weight of the *Sharia*—the religious laws.

'Along about Kosti we come to the sea change in Sudan,' Harry explained. 'We're coming into the flood plain of the White Nile, and the Moslem tribes are giving way to the southern Sudanese black tribes—the animists and the Christians. And the farther south we go from Kosti, the closer we get to the war.'

'War! I thought the war was over!' War was something Mattie hadn't counted on. A straight management or engineering problem was right down her alley. But war? She remembered the stories her sister Becky had told about the war in Chad.

'There's nothing funny about war,' she grumbled. 'What are they fighting for?'

'Freedom,' said Harry casually. 'Booty. Power. Religion. Independence. Take your pick. Sudan never *was* a united state, despite all the efforts of the colonial powers. They completely ignored tribal boundaries—and tribes is what Sudan is all about. Since the overthrow of President Nimeiri, the new government has reneged on promises of autonomy for the south, and has brought in Libyan troops as allies. The pastoral tribes—especially the Dinka—are up in revolt. The government holds all the cities; the rebels hold all the roads and waterways. I hear they actually shot down a government plane over Malakal the other day. How about that? They've jumped from spears to anti-aircraft rockets in one decade. It scares the hell out of me, little lady. Hey, there we go.'

While they were talking the sun had gone down, and directly ahead of them, on both sides of the river, there were lights. Some flares, some lanterns, some which actually burned uniformly, as if they might be electric. Harry helped Mattie up to her feet.

'Kosti,' he announced grandly, then qualified, 'Well, it's not all that big, and it *does* look better at night—you can't see all the junk.'

'I don't care how small or rusty it is,' she groaned. 'Just so long as it has a hot shower and a soft bed. The sooner I finish this problem, the happier I'll be.'

'Not to worry,' he laughed. 'We have a fine guest-house. You'll enjoy it.'

'Give me leave to doubt,' she cautioned him, and grabbed for the rail as the *Falashi* ran into the side of the pier with more enthusiasm than common sense, throwing half the passengers off their feet. Ryan Quinn loomed up out of the darkness and, without a word, slung his pack over one shoulder and motioned towards the gangplank.

'Before we go ashore,' Mattie said as sweetly as she could manage, 'I want to thank you, Mr Quinn, for the use of your bedroll.' And how's that, Ryan Quinn, for the first application of the needle? She was so pleased with herself that she failed to notice his grin hiding in the darkness.

'Not at all, *Mattie*,' he rumbled. 'On second thoughts, please make yourself at home in my bed whenever the occasion presents itself.' There was no mistaking the sarcasm, and her face turned red.

She turned her back on him and threw a chilly 'thank you' over her shoulder as she stalked off. It might have all come off well, except that the ship was tied up more than four feet away from the dock, and this time the gangplank consisted of a single plank, only three feet wide. Nervousness was Mattie's undoing, nervousness and the hulk of man who stepped on the plank directly behind her. The wood vibrated with his weight and shifted her to one side, with one foot poised half on and half off the secure area. She squeaked a little alarm, almost smothered with fear. His hand caught her elbow before she lost her footing, swinging her back to the centre of the plank, and safety.

Mattie rocked back and forth for a moment, fighting off the impulse to throw herself into his arms. Rage was the only answer. I wouldn't have been that close to falling off if he hadn't stepped on the gangplank, she told herself fiercely. So it's all his fault! Which allowed her to build up a sufficient head of anger to shake herself loose from his hand when her feet hit the solid dock. She might have said any one of a dozen things, but he had seen the look on her face in the light of the flares, and moved smartly away from her, leaving to Harry Crampton all the little necessities of landing.

The jeep waiting for them at the base of the pier was an old one, and dusty. Harry looked a little apologetic. 'I'm responsible for fleet maintenance,' he offered.

'It looks fine to me,' Mattie told him. 'All it has to do to make me happy is keep running. Besides, the sand has carved some very attractive patterns on the hood.' She took a front seat to emphasise her position, expecting the enigmatic Mr Quinn to scramble around her into the back. Instead Ryan Quinn took the driver's seat, still without saying a word, then looked a challenge at her. Caught between anger and her long training in politeness, she glared wordlessly at him, then scrambled into the back so that Harry, considerably older than either of them and probably not as mobile, could have the comfortable seat.

'Thank you, Mattie,' the older man said as he sat down. 'I'm beyond the age when bone-crushing back seats are attractive.' All of which brought a bark of derision from Ryan Quinn as he put the vehicle into four-wheel drive and snapped her head back with the speed of his start. They stopped at the entrance to the bridge. The town behind them was almost silent. In the light of flares Mattie could see a dozen steamers tied up at the docks, all far more palatial than the *Falashi*.

Harry caught the direction of her stare. 'They haven't moved a ship south for months,' he shouted at her. 'It used to be you could ride all the way from Kosti, over a thousand miles south to Juba, but no more. The rebels control the river passage. Nothing moves.' As he described how things might have been, a pair of soldiers were checking all their travel permits. They made some point in Arabic, and Ryan stifled their argument with a few pungent words—words that Mattie could not remember hearing in her language class. The guards waved the jeep reluctantly forward.

'Now this bridge,' Harry called back to her, 'is the Latimore bridge. Designed for trains, but can carry cars or wagons or camel caravans at need. Third bridge on this site in ten years, this is.'

'What happened to the others?' she shouted back at him.

'Blown up,' he reported, gesturing towards the supports on the western side. 'Victims of the war! That's why we have that detachment of soldiers down there.'

They didn't look much like soldiers, despite the fact that they wore camouflage-green uniforms. None of them stirred as the jeep raced over the bridge and went bouncing down on to the sandy left bank.

All around them were dispersal railroad tracks loaded with boxcars and hopper cars. 'This is the railroad yard?' Mattie exclaimed. A herd of battered steam locomotives stood head to tail, their paint peeling, their driver-wheels showing rust.

'Had to build it here,' Harry returned. 'We can't move them forwards, and they won't go back!'

'I'll have to see about that,' she muttered. Ryan must have had very good hearing, for, despite the rattle of the vehicle and the whistle of the wind, he laughed.

The Latimore camp was about a quarter of a mile from the end of the bridge, on higher ground, and built according to the company manual. Rows of comfortable barracks and cottages were built in a fortress-like square, surrounded by an empty spotlighted area, and a high, barbed-wire fence. The guard on the gate was not a soldier; instead he was a tall, naked, Nubian warrior, armed with the traditional spear. A man over six foot six, almost as black as the night, he gave a stern, primitive touch to the electrically lit camp he guarded. The jeep stopped, and Ryan exchanged a few words with him in a dialect Mattie could not even name. Moments later they were parked in front of the headquarters building.

Mattie struggled out of the jeep last, feeling to the fullest the result of a night sleeping on a steel deck, six days of wandering through the maze of bureaucracy in Khartoum, two days of partial starvation, and the mental and physical drain she had experienced in the uneasy presence of Ryan Quinn.

Two people were waiting for them on the wide steps. One, an Arab Sudanese in full dress, came running down the steps with a grin on his face. Mattie was too tired to look beyond him into the light.

'Ahmed bin Raschid,' he introduced himself, with a big smile that revealed fine white teeth. He pronounced his name as if it were written with a German 'ch' sound— 'Achmed'. It added just the right touch. Mattie offered him a medium-level smile and held out her hand.

'Mathilda Latimore,' she said softly. *'Sala'am aleikum.'*

'Ah.' His round olive face lit up. 'You speak the language of Islam!'

'Only a few words,' she protested. His laugh was infectious, he was altogether good-looking, and Ryan Quinn immediately threw cold water over her enthusiasm.

'Ahmed is the government representative,' he commented. He didn't need to say any more. Mattie had been on many a foreign contract, where the 'government representative' meant spy, secret police, and often master shakedown artist. Mattie struggled to reclaim her hand, which Ahmed was reluctant to turn loose as they went up the four steps that led to the wide veranda.

She had her head down as they climbed. All she knew of the surprise was announced by the sudden cessation of conversation ahead of her. There was a moment of silence and a shuffling of feet, then Ryan Quinn's deep, angry voice.

'Virginia—what the hell are *you* doing here?'

Mattie's head snapped up. The woman standing outlined in the light was a slender, well-shaped creature dressed in the finest silk dinner dress, a smooth, golden flow that emphasised bust and hips and fell gracefully down to her ankles. Her dark hair was extravagantly piled high on her head, leaving the shadows and planes of her thin face to stand alone. An earring hung suspended from one ear, a long, thin, golden thing with an inscribed figure that Mattie could not clearly see. Not a beautiful woman, but a commanding, handsome one. And a worried woman. She wore a smile on her face, but had a tear glistening in her eye.

The party flowed into the building, Ryan leading, walking stiffly beside the woman. Harry walked alone behind them, and Mattie followed, with Ahmed almost attached to her side. They turned into a large meeting room and bar. Ryan Quinn went directly to the bar, poured himself a double shot of straight Scotch, and threw it down his throat in one motion. He set his glass down on the bar with a thump, locked both hands on the rolled front of the bar itself, then turned around.

Mattie watched him like a hawk. When he turned, his face was bland. The terrible anger was gone, and he even managed a little smile. 'Harry, Miss Latimore, Ahmed,' he announced, 'may I present my wife—I mean, my former wife, Virginia.'

'Good lord!' muttered Harry, and brushed his way past everyone to try his hand at the bottle. Virginia Quinn stood frozen in position for another second or two, then with a harsh shout—half-victory, half-pain—she ran at Ryan and threw her arms around his neck.

'Oh, Ryan!' she moaned.

'Harry,' called Mattie, 'I'm about to die of hunger and thirst, and I need a shower so badly that it hurts!' Harry came over to her, a morose look on his face, a glass in his hand. 'And besides, I think the three of us are remarkably *de trop*,' she said softly.

Each of the men offered her an arm. She went out of the room with her two gallants, struggling not to look over her shoulder, feeling very upset. My stomach, she told herself as they led her into the kitchen. Something I ate—or didn't eat. It's got nothing to do with Ryan Quinn!

'There's a lavatory behind that red door.' Harry pointed her in the right direction. 'We have equal-opportunity bathrooms here. Why don't you take a little time to wash? I'll lay hands on what's available, and scrounge us a plateful of sandwiches. There's no cook on duty until morning.'

'You mean, I look that bad?' she sighed.

'Not so,' enthused Ahmed. 'You look a little— rumpled, but the real you shines through.'

'I hope not.' Mattie grinned at both of them and headed for the red door. 'My *real* self is more Dragon Lady than Sleeping Beauty.'

Like all things in the corporation, it was a standard bathroom, gleaming pristine white fixtures, clean enough so you could eat off the floor. Nothing was more important to Bruce Latimore than that his employees, wherever they worked, had the best food, the most sanitary surroundings. A district manager might push a road forward at twice the contract speed, but if his bathrooms were dirty he was gone.

Mattie needed only one look in the mirror to confirm her worst fears. Her hair had been crushed and blown and tousled, and looked very much like a nest for a family of fieldmice. There was enough soot on her face from the *Falashi*'s crooked smokestack to require a chimney sweep's support. Her skirt was twisted around sideways, and her safari jacket would have been banned in Boston. She shrugged her shoulders, slipped out of the jacket, and filled a bowl with hot water.

Fifteen minutes later, things had improved. Her hair was in some order, hanging down neatly to her shoulders, its forward strands curling very slightly inward towards her cheeks, thanks to a sterilised comb she had found in one of the cabinets. Her skirt had been sponged and set straight, her face was rosy from the scrubbing, but clean. Only the safari jacket was beyond recall. It was wrinkled, dirty, sweaty—and because she hadn't thought to wear anything under it, she had to put it back on. She made a little moue at herself in the mirror.

The two men were sitting across the table from each other when she came back out. Ahmed sprang to his feet; Harry shifted his weight, winked at her, and settled back. Too much of a good thing, Mattie thought, as the Arab helped her into a chair. There was a platter full of sandwiches in the middle of the table.

'Beer?' offered Harry.

'I thought you'd never ask,' she chuckled. 'What's hiding between these pieces of bread?'

'Various kinds of meat,' he fudged. 'You'll like them.' To prove his honesty, he took the top one off the pile and began to chew it. Ahmed, a little more fastidious, broke a sandwich in half and nibbled at it gently.

Mattie's hunger was too great. She dived in, taking one cautious bite, liking the taste, slugging at the beer bottle beside her and then chewing away.

'No glasses for ladies,' she teased as she went back to the beer bottle.

'Never had any ladies here before,' Harry commented sadly. 'And now we have two. Makes a little problem.'

'It can't be all that bad,' she returned. 'I—what arrangements do we have for the night?'

'We have one special bungalow for female visitors,' Harry told her. 'Never been used. I sent a man over to check it out. You'll spend the night in comfort.'

'Thank God!' sighed Mattie. 'Say, this is good. Tastes like lamb?'

'Pretty close,' Ahmed laughed—a high-pitched laugh, with the taste of cruelty in it. I don't like this man, Mattie told herself. I just don't like this man! She turned away from him.

'How close, Harry?'

'Straight from the hip?'

'What else?'

'So OK. Young camel. It's a local delicacy. Most of the camels are driven to Egypt and sold at premium prices. They have camel drives the way América once had cattle drives—make the beasts walk all the way to the slaughterhouse.'

'No beef in the Sudan?'

'Don't say that around here,' Ahmed commanded harshly. 'The central government has plenty of trouble with cattle!'

'Now what have I said wrong?' Mattie asked. 'Dear God, every time I open my mouth I put my foot in it!'

'Don't let it get to you.' Harry reached for another sandwich. 'There's plenty of beef in these parts, but the native tribes count them as wealth. The only time one gets eaten is at a special festival—or occasionally when they get too old to function.'

'Sacred cows, as in India?'

'No, not that. Their cattle are money to them. Cattle are their unit of exchange. A man's herd is his bank account. You don't go around eating ten-dollar bills, do you? The local tribesmen don't go around eating their cattle, either. Unless they're hard up.'

'Oh, brother!' sighed Mattie. 'I thought I'd studied up on the situation before I came over, but they told me all the wrong things in my final briefing.' She barely managed to stifle a yawn. 'You know, I don't think I can make it. How about somebody pointing me towards this honeymoon cottage? I'll take a couple of those sandwiches with me—and another bottle of beer?'

Ahmed did the honours, carrying her food as he led her out on to the veranda and down the stairs. The moon was high, but could not compete with the search-lights that scattered the night. The bungalow was a simple affair in the next block down from the administration building. The door was not locked. Ahmed led Mattie into the living-room and set her sandwiches down on the table.

'One shower, one kitchen, one bedroom——' he demonstrated, throwing the doors open. The bedroom was fairly spacious, and held two single beds.

'Thank you.' She did her best to usher him politely out of the door. He didn't plan to co-operate. 'What is it you *want*?' she finally snapped at him.

'What do I want?' he laughed. 'A beautiful girl, a moonlit night? I want to share your *makhadda*, little brown dove.' He was smiling gently as he came at her.

Mattie had had enough of *this* situation. When he was within inches of her, her right fist, doubled tight, stabbed across that short distance and plunged deep into his solar plexus. His smile disappeared as the air 'whouffed' out of his lungs and he doubled over, hands folded over the injury.

'Listen here, sheikh,' said Mattie grimly, 'I don't share my pillow with anyone. *Imshi!* Get out!' Ahmed wobbled towards the door, which she held open. She helped him along his path with a good shove, which pitched the Sudanese man directly into a dark shadow standing outside, who added to his speed.

'Have a little trouble, did you?' Ryan Quinn asked pleasantly. Good lord, he's actually smiling, Mattie thought. That's a first! Of course, he's got one arm around his wife. Reconciliation?

'Nothing I couldn't handle,' she mumbled. 'I need a night's sleep. What do you want?'

'Not very hospitable,' he observed. 'You *do* have a bad temper.'

'Why, you——' she raged. 'I ought to——'

'Hey, I give up!' He stepped back from the door, warding her off with one hand. 'It's something I heard your father say at a family dinner. You were away, and he was giving a run-down of the family.'

'Yeah? Funny you'd say that,' she retorted. 'And what did my mother say?'

He looked down at her quizzically. 'You know, I never gave that a thought. And nobody ever mentioned you were a female. It was all Mattie this and Mattie that. Your mother—the little lady?'

'Yes, the little lady.'

'She said something like "Now, Bruce," and your father changed the subject.'

'So maybe you *did* hear it,' Mattie admitted. 'Now, what do you want with me?'

'Nothing, really,' he said. 'But since there's only one bungalow for female guests, you and Virginia are going to have to share until I can make other arrangements!'

Mattie, her jaw hanging open, stepped aside as the pair of them came into the house. She watched while they kissed. Not a passionate kiss, but it might have been very satisfactory, Mattie found herself thinking. Other arrangements? Why didn't he just take the woman to his bed directly? What the devil am I mixed up in now?

Whatever it was, Ryan Quinn was not about to tell her. He patted his former wife on the shoulder and walked back out. As he passed Mattie, still standing and holding the door half open, he chucked her gently under the chin and laughed.

'Goodnight, boss,' he mocked, and was gone before she could think of a suitable answer.

CHAPTER THREE

THE MEETING was held in the big conference room two days after her arrival. Mattie had spent most of the intervening time sleeping. Her mental clock had not yet adjusted to Sudanese time, and the business of sharing a bungalow with Virginia Quinn had proved not too comfortable.

'Always complaining,' she whispered to Harry, who sat next to her. 'What the devil do you suppose brought her all the way out here?'

'Money,' Harry returned. 'She's bled him dry for years, and now she wants more.'

'Child support?'

He shook his head. 'They don't have any children. What's she complaining about?'

Mattie shrugged her shoulders. It wasn't something she wanted to tell anyone. She had been sitting in the living-room of the bungalow just before dinner the previous night, thumbing through a six-month-old *Newsweek* magazine, when Virginia Quinn slammed her way into the house. The fragile little brunette, her fists clenched, paced up and down the room, agitated, then stopped in front of Mattie. There were tears in her eyes— tears of frustration.

'You're his boss,' she accused Mattie.

'In a sense, yes—I'm the vice-president of the corporation. But as far as operations here in Africa are concerned, Ryan is his own boss.'

'Ryan, is it?' The brunette hopped on the oversight immediately. 'You and he have something going, haven't

46

you?' The woman's voice rose to a shrill peak. 'You *want* my husband!' Her clenched hands batted at the table-top in a hysterical rhythm.

Oh, lord, Mattie thought, I'm caged up with a psychotic! 'First of all,' she said calmly, 'I understood you were divorced. Secondly, I wouldn't have that gorilla if they were giving him away for shopping coupons!'

'You can't fool me!' Virginia shrieked. 'I know how you women run after Ryan!' She stopped to breathe, struggled with herself, and regained control. 'There's no use chasing him,' she said softly, sounding more menacing than when she had been screaming. 'He's mine. We were married in hell, and the chains are still fastened!'

'I'm sorry to hear that,' Mattie returned gently. 'It must be difficult——'

'Of course it's difficult,' Virginia interrupted. 'The man's an immoral bastard, but he's still mine!'

'I—can't believe that of Mr Quinn,' Mattie protested. 'I'm sure he must have been difficult to live with, but——'

'What do you know?' Virginia spat at her. 'Brought up with a silver spoon, you were—that's what I hear. What do you know about grubbing around at the bottom of the heap?'

Mattie sighed. 'Is there anything I can do to help?'

'Besides keeping your hands off him?' the other woman queried. 'Yes, there *is* something you can do, for both of us. Tear up his contract and write him a new one at twice the salary. He's worth every cent of it, and I need the money—now!'

'That's something I can't control,' Mattie told her. 'The board would have to meet and discuss it. I *can* let my father know, if you feel that would help.'

'God, you good-hearted people make me sick!' Virginia returned as she slammed her way into the bedroom. A bottle clinked against a glass, and the smell of whisky floated through the little house. Mattie shook her head; people who found solace in a bottle got little sympathy from her.

People were filtering into the room one at a time. She knew none of them, and none of them knew her. They would come in, stand just inside the door, and look around to spot this 'boss woman' who had come to turn things upside-down. She could tell when they located her. Their eyes opened wide at the 'child' of the Latimore family, then they would blink and hurry around the conference table to the most inconspicuous seat. Mattie did her best to catalogue them. It was a fun game, and her usual percentage of accuracy was less than twenty-five.

In any event, she was not watching in the right direction. The seat to her right was suddenly pulled out, and Ryan Quinn plumped himself down and leaned over towards her. 'You'll have to be careful,' he whispered. 'I understand your problem, but you did a dangerous thing the other night.'

'Dangerous? What?'

'With young Ahmed,' he returned. 'The story is all over the compound. He's lost a great deal of face, and for a government official, that's bad news.'

'Face!' she snorted. 'What was I supposed to do—lie down and let him rape me?'

'I don't have any answers,' Ryan said quietly. 'But you need to know that young Ahmed is the voice of the government in Kosti, and he has the soldiers to back him up. Like any snake, he's dangerous when crossed, and you crossed him in the worst way. Sudanese military men are very macho.'

'And what do you suggest I do about it?' she asked stiffly. 'Run away home to Daddy?'

A little grin tugged at the corners of his mouth. 'I'll say this for you, Miss Latimore, you've got a lot of guts.' The compliment so surprised Mattie that she was caught in the middle of a breath, and held it. And then he punctured her balloon. 'For a woman, that is. It might not be a bad idea to run. I can get you on the train tonight. Interested?'

'No, I'm *not* interested!' she snapped at him. 'Latimores don't run. I intend to do my job, Mr Quinn.' He glared back at her for a moment, then smiled. He needs taking down a peg or two, Mattie decided. 'Besides,' she added, 'I wouldn't miss rooming with your— wife—for anything in the world. She has some delightful stories to tell!'

'Damn you!' He wheeled his chair away from her and rapped on the table. A silence fell over the room. Mattie watched as his cheeks coloured in anger. She could see the pulse-point on his neck wildly beating, and had the crazy notion that she should lean over and touch it. But the momentary insanity passed.

'George,' he rumbled, 'begin with the situation— please.' The last word dropped like an icicle and seemed to shatter on the table. The young man at the far end of the table struggled up and went over to the map board.

'The railroad follows the road.' He demonstrated with a light-pointer. 'From Kosti to El Obeid, and from there rising uphill until it gets to Darfur Province, on the border with Chad. You should notice that this makes the railroad the boundary line between the Masakin tribes, here to the south, and the Arab Kababish tribes, to the north.' He flipped a more detailed map down over the first. He went on for twenty minutes, crossing every T and dotting every I. Ten minutes into his lecture Mattie began to itch. At the fifteen-minute mark her foot began to tap. At the twentieth minute she had had enough. Her little fist rapped on the table.

'Mr——?' she interrupted.

'Jensen,' Ryan volunteered. 'From our operations department.'

'Er—yes—Mr Jensen,' she sighed, 'I fear you're telling me more than I care to know about this railroad. Just get to the bottom line, please.'

The engineer threw a hopeful look at Ryan, received no indication of support, and almost choked himself on a glass of water.

'Well,' he admitted, 'our first problem was to replace seventeen culverts which were washed out by the floods of last year, when the drought broke. Today these three culverts are still down.' His pointer designated three areas, separated from each other by about four miles, to the west of El Obeid.'

'Mr Jensen, surely it wouldn't take a great deal of time to repair three culverts? You could assign a crew to each one, put them on double time, and stand back to let the dirt fly?'

Jensen looked warily at Ryan. Out of the corner of her eye, Mattie saw him nod.

'We've done that—three times,' Jensen said gravely, and Mattie felt a little chill run up her spine. Three times? That could only mean——

'Sabotage?' she asked grimly.

'Sabotage,' the big man next to her echoed. 'Frank?'

Another man stood up, half-way down the table. 'All our locomotive engineers have refused to move an engine past Er Rahad,' he said. 'In fact, about half of them have developed serious illness at home, and have already left. The others are sitting on their hands. We haven't rolled a train west in twelve days.'

'But the soldiers——' Mattie protested, only to be greeted by laughter.

'You still don't understand,' Ryan said gravely. 'The soldiers aren't here to protect the line, or to protect us, for that matter. The soldiers are here to rule Kosti, to collect taxes, to control the graft in town. They won't stir out of their camps. Do you have any other questions, Miss Vice-President?'

Mattie took a deep breath. 'Yes, several,' she said firmly. 'First of all, who's doing all this?'

'That one's easy,' Jensen retorted. 'It's the young Masakin warriors. They're out of the control of their elders.'

'And then the second has to be—*why?*'

'There's no need for us to keep these men from their work,' Ryan interjected. 'Let's you and me take a little ride in the country and talk about it.'

'We could talk just as well in here,' she snapped.

'Yes, but riding in a jeep, we can be sure nobody is listening at the keyhole,' he murmured.

Ryan brought the jeep to a halt on the top of the hill, and turned off the engine. Before them, stretching north and east, were the beginnings of the fruitful plains, the White Nile, and Kosti. The hill itself was but a mound, not one of the real foothills that extended west and south of them, towards Koalib, the mountain of Nuba, some four thousand, three hundred feet above sea level.

The sere grass was thin on the ground; poor grazing land, but still not a desert. A single old baobab tree lifted sturdy limbs over their heads and provided the only shade within miles.

The air was thick and hot, the mid-afternoon temperature holding at a hundred and five degrees. 'This air—you could almost eat it with a spoon,' complained Mattie, climbing stiffly out of her seat.

'But you *do* feel a little cooler?' Part of their tour had taken them down into the *sukh* in Kosti, where dozens of Arab merchants used the streets as extensions of their little shops.

Now Mattie wore a light wide-brimmed bush hat to replace the heavier pith helmet. The safari jacket had given way to a simple white cotton blouse with a high collar and long sleeves which fitted loosely over the top of her wrap-around skirt. Under the blouse was a loose-fitting cotton camisole, also white.

'No constricting clothing,' Ryan insisted. 'Leave plenty of room for air to circulate, but don't expose too much skin. You need to keep the insects off you. And white, because that colour reflects the sun. Haven't you noticed that most of the natives wear white?'

'I just thought it was a preferred colour,' she mumbled, 'or maybe some religious thing.'

'Well, it's not,' he affirmed as they pushed their way through the crowds. The crowds themselves would have been memorable, but the fact that he *smiled* made it all even more so. Mattie stored the idea away in the back of her mind.

She had accumulated a complete wardrobe, including half a dozen colourful *dishdash*, the simple but more widely cut form of the *djellaba*. 'Made of Sudanese cotton,' Ryan explained, 'in Sudanese textile mills, but according to Yemeni design. Why so many?'

'I have three sisters,' she explained, 'and a mother who loves presents.'

'Nothing but girls in the family?'

'Oh, lord, no,' she laughed. 'Michael is twelve now—he's the baby of the family.'

'Your mother's been kept busy.'

'It's too complicated to explain,' she sighed. 'Where do we look next?'

'It's time we had that talk,' drawled Ryan, and drove them back over the river, out along the road towards El Obeid, and up the little hill.

'Are you thirsty?' He handed her the big evaporative canteen which had been hanging over the radiator of the jeep, cooling itself by the passage of wind and the evaporation of the slightest bit of moisture that it purposefully leaked.

'Love it,' murmured Mattie, but when she put it to her mouth she remembered sister Becky's lectures, and took only a few small sips. When she handed it back, Ryan was grinning—as if she had passed another test, done something right for a change.

He took a similar tasting and screwed the cap down tight again. 'You know, you've not only got guts, but you're not as stupid as I thought,' he declared.

'Well, thank *you* very much,' she returned huffily.

'Hey, I didn't mean it that way,' he protested. 'Honestly, I meant it as a compliment. I'm just out of practice in good society.'

'How long have you been out in Africa?' she asked.

He pulled off his bush hat and wiped his forehead with the kerchief he wore around his neck. She followed suit. 'This time, perhaps six years,' he told her.

'Where is home, and how often have you gone there in that time?'

'You're a persistent thing, aren't you? Vernon, Texas, is where I hang my hat, but I haven't been there in all that time. I take vacations. Dakar, Cairo, Istanbul— those sorts of places.'

'That's a long time to be away,' she said sympathetically. 'I guess it could have a strange effect on a man.'

'Does that mean you accept my apology?'

'Well, if you made one, I certainly accept,' she returned. 'But it wasn't necessary, you know. We're business partners, not socialites. Now, you were about to say something confidential. Is there some reason why we couldn't talk in camp?'

Ryan sank back on to the jeep seat and flexed his tired shoulders. 'The walls of our camp are porous,' he sighed. 'It generally takes about ten minutes for our decisions to reach the government camp, and maybe ten more before every merchant in Kosti knows all about it. It makes it hard to conduct business.'

'You can't filter out the spies?'

'Not a chance.' Ryan shook his head in disgust. 'The servants are all provided by the government. We can't fire them—and they know who they work for. All except the camp guards—we hire them independently. We have one contingent of Nuba, and another from the Nuer tribe.'

'So, all right,' said Mattie cheerfully, 'unless that vulture up there is equipped with a camera, we're alone. What is it you wanted to talk about?'

'This whole ball of wax,' he grunted. 'The railroad, the operation, the graft, the government—everything.'

'For this, I'll sit down,' Mattie returned, climbing back into the jeep. 'Go ahead.'

'What we have at first blush is the fact that the Masakin tribes are disrupting the railroad,' Ryan began. 'That's absolutely true. What we try not to mention is that the railroad and the road are built across the northern part of their ancient lands. The construction makes it impossible for the Masakin to graze their herds northwards. At the same time it's added grazing lands to the Kababish, a Moslem tribe up north. Now, in case you haven't noticed, the government of Sudan is

Moslem. Not too many of the black tribes are represented. All right so far?'

'Easy enough, is there a quiz to follow?'

He looked at her thoughtfully and pulled out pipe and tobacco. 'It gets more complicated,' he continued. 'You'll find that every tribe down in these parts has a small military detachment of Moslems assigned to them. Just as our Ahmed controls Kosti, so these little units are trying to bring the black tribes under control. That's one irritant the Masakin have to put up with. Now, next. South of the Nuba lands are one branch of Nuer. Here, let me make you a sketch.' He climbed out of the jeep, cleared a piece of grassland, and drew a diagram in the sandy soil with his pencil.

'Like this, now. The Moslem Kababish to the north, and a piece of the Masakin grazing land available to them. The Masakin in the middle, unable to herd north because of the railroad, and nagged by a government military group. And south here, the Nuer. The Nuer represent a new thing in this part of the world. A major company has found oil in their lands. The Nuer still count their wealth in cattle, but they also work as hardhats for the oil company, and can afford to buy more cattle—more wealth. Now, since they have more cattle—more wealth—they have to find a place to graze them, and so the Nuer are pushing northwards into Masakin land. And there you go. In summary, the total of Sudan's problems: religion, grazing lands, new wealth, old customs, and a new Moslem government trying to unify the land.'

'And *we* built the railroad?' Mattie gasped. 'Good God, what were we thinking of?'

'Well now, we're absolved of *that* sin,' laughed Ryan. 'We didn't *build* the railroad, we only repaired it! What do you think?'

'What I think——' she started to say, then looked up at him, grinning. 'You don't suppose we could build rafts and float the entire Latimore crew downstream into Egypt?'

He gave her a startled look, a look that made him appear to be really *human*, and she caught at his hand and laughed. 'The Latimore humour is noted for being zany,' she explained gently, but he wasn't listening. He was staring down at where her little hand had disappeared into his. Looking, and then gently squeezing, as if it had been years since he accepted the companionship of touching.

'No, what I really wanted to say,' Mattie fumbled, 'is that we need some way to connect up with the Masakin leadership. You said earlier that the young warriors have broken loose from the control of their elders?'

'Maybe,' he returned, still clutching at her hand. 'And then again, maybe not. These people may be primitive, but they're not stupid. This whole thing might very well be a plan concocted by Artafi and his council.'

'Artafi?'

'Yeah. The old gentleman who's the super-chieftain of the Masakin tribe. *They* call him king. The people of Khartoum don't like that.'

'You know him?'

'We've met.'

'Well, for goodness' sakes,' she exclaimed excitedly, 'let's get in contact with him and see if we can't make a deal!'

Ryan stretched and looked down at her solemnly. 'You make it sound so simple, lady. Where the hell do you think I've been for the past thirty days? Standing outside the council chamber of the Masakin trying to get an audience! Not a chance. They won't listen.'

'So maybe they have a protocol,' Mattie objected. 'I'm the vice-president of Latimore. You must have some contacts. Arrange for *me* to talk to their council.'

'Nothing is ever easy in Africa,' he said sombrely. 'I don't know any way in the world that I could get *you* into the chamber.'

'There's no such thing as *never*,' she said firmly. 'All you need is a fresh approach.'

'Oh, you bet,' he snapped, dropping her hand abruptly. 'All we need—lady, you haven't the faintest idea what you're asking.'

'That's possible,' she told him coolly, but her attitude belied the words. 'So, since you know so much more than I do, perhaps you could explain it all—in tiny words, of course, so as not to strain my capabilities.'

'I'd like to strain your——' muttered Ryan. Mattie looked down to where his hands were clenching and un- clenching. Around my throat, she thought, that's where he'd like them! She offered him a perky little smile and shrugged her shoulders. 'Speak freely. I really want to understand.'

'The hell you do!' he roared. 'Sit down and let me explain a few thousand facts of life to you.'

She walked away from him to the edge of the shaded area, wrapped her arms around herself, and shivered. There was something about this man that just rubbed her the wrong way, until now it was assuming the pro- portion of an Egyptian pyramid. Roaring at her!

'What is it?' Softly said, at her elbow. Mattie looked around at him. Concern, honest concern sparked at her from Ryan's eyes. His hand took her elbow gently, soothingly. 'I didn't mean to scare you half to death,' he said anxiously. 'I guess—I'm not cut out for dealing with—women.'

'It's something you'll have to learn,' she returned bitterly. 'I just hadn't realised how little prepared I was for this—this whole continent. Well——' She unfolded her arms gradually, then smiled at him.

'I'm glad we're all alone,' she said cheerfully. 'I'm about to say something nice about you—and I wouldn't want it to get around.'

'Me neither,' he laughed. 'I *do* have a certain reputation to maintain.'

'Well, despite all that, Ryan Quinn, you're a hell of a fellow to have around when things aren't going well. Now, what were you going to tell me?'

He shook his head and chuckled under his breath. 'My first compliment in my whole life,' he told her, 'and I'm about to break it wide open. Are you sure you want to hear this?'

'If the Masakin are breaking up our railroad I intend to see them and make some kind of a deal,' Mattie said firmly. 'And the sooner done, the better. Now, please go ahead with the explanation. The quicker I get this out of the way, the sooner I can get back to Boston.'

'OK. So it goes like this. The Masakin have certain customs that are—a little strange to Bostonians.'

'I'll bet they do!' she rejoined.

'No sarcasm, lady. Their culture is a mixture between fixed agriculture and wandering grazing. A Masakin lad goes off cattle-herding when he's ten years old. Before then he works in the village. Sometimes he'll follow the herds for as much as six months without ever getting back home. He keeps this up until he's thirty-five. There's a ceremony in which he's inducted into the organisation of elders. At that time he gets married, becomes a member of the council, settles down in the village, and never has to go off again.'

'I—really don't care for an exposition of their sex life,' Mattie reminded him. 'How about if you just point out the key words?'

'No sweat. The key words are: married—councillor—elders. Got that?'

'I've got the words, but not the music. Maybe you'd better play that over again.'

'OK.' Ryan stopped to fiddle with his pipe again. But he's not loading it, and he's not lighting it, Mattie thought, so just what the devil is he doing with it? Killing time? Fumbling for the right words? Or maybe he's just come to the punch line? The one I'm not going to like?

'To simplify,' he continued, 'in order for me to go before the councillors of the tribe and be heard, I must be first a member of the elders—that's an age problem in which I just qualify. And second, I have to be married!'

Her eyes opened wide, lifting her eyebrows comically. 'But——' she spluttered, 'I—don't see what the problem is. You *are* married, and by some lucky chance your wife is right here in Kosti! As far as I can see, we've got it made. Why don't you——'

'You still don't understand,' he grumbled. 'First of all, I'm *not* married, and haven't been for six years. Secondly, that's well known around these parts. The bush telegraph is a lot more efficient than telephones and satellites.'

'So you could fake it,' Mattie said wryly. 'I had a long talk with your wife. I beg your pardon—a long listen with your wife. I'm sure she'd be glad to reinstate you, and pose as your loving little wifey.'

'Oh, God,' he muttered, and banged the hood of the jeep with his clenched fist. 'Why me, God?'

Mattie grinned. In her twenty-five years she had spent little time exploring the male animal. This one was not the least bit like Pop, and indeed a long way from being like Becky's husband, Jake. *All I have to do,* she assured herself, *is to keep emotionally uninvolved with the Quinn family, and I'll learn a bundle about people!*

'You don't have to enjoy yourself so much,' Ryan muttered.

'Oh, I'm not,' she lied. 'I'm very concerned! It's all very important—not only to me personally but to Latimore Incorporated.'

'I'm glad you think so,' he growled. 'Now, kindly wipe that smirk off your face and listen. I can't possibly take Virginia with me. About twenty minutes into the scene she'd have a fit, scream her head off, and demand to be flown directly to Cairo. My wife—my former wife—in case you haven't noticed it, is not quite all there.'

'Oh, temperamental,' Mattie agreed cautiously. 'But I wouldn't go so far as to say——'

'Well, believe me, she is,' he shouted, then suddenly slammed one fist into the other hand and struggled to control himself. 'Damn! I *swore* I wouldn't roar at you. Why is it? You agitate me more than any woman I've ever met, Mattie Latimore. There have been times in the last two or three days that I've wanted to throw you overboard, and other times when I—oh, what the hell! I've blown the whole programme already, so I might as well do what I've wanted to do all the time!'

Before she could duck out of the way, his two big ham-sized hands landed on her shoulders and pulled her hard up against his iron frame. Like all the Latimore girls, Mattie had had her share of karate lessons, but this bear of a man gave her no chance to exercise technique. He pulled her in, wrapped her up, and when she tried to kick his shinbone he lifted her off the ground, until they were eye to eye. And Mattie didn't care for what she saw in those eyes.

'Don't you dare!' she gritted at him.

'Oh, I dare, all right,' he muttered. His mouth came down on hers. She wriggled her head from side to side, but there was no escape. His cool, moist lips sealed her mouth, locked her head in position, and made all her protests useless. Well, at least it isn't rape, she told herself.

It was all she had time for, that one little crazy thought. The pressure eased, and for some reason she no longer *cared* to escape. Like a soft invasion, Ryan teased and tantalised her lips, making her like what she did not like. Only when he switched to her earlobe did she complain. His unshaven cheek scratched across her soft skin, and she rebelled. He set her down on the ground, far enough away so he could avoid any damage she might work up to.

There's something wrong here, her analytical mind told her. You obviously don't have all the facts. What's missing? You've been kissed before, girl. What are you overlooking that's causing you to be so—upset? No, more like frustrated! Nothing came to mind. Collect more data, her internal computer suggested.

'Now then,' she said calmly, 'if the wrestling match is over, perhaps we could get back to business.'

'Your cheek is all red,' said Ryan, and reached out to touch the place, but she flinched away from him.

'Of course it's red,' she said harshly. 'You didn't shave!'

'Hey, I *am* sorry.' He took a step in her direction, and she promptly backed off.

'Let me see if I have this clearly,' she told him. 'You went up to the Masakin tribal area, and they wouldn't give you a hearing because you're not married, and are therefore not qualified to advise?'

'That's about it,' he muttered.

'And what is it that keeps *me* from going up there to advise them?'

'Oh, lord,' he muttered, 'you haven't been listening between the lines, lady. Women—married or not—are *never* allowed in the council. Not even the queen. Never!'

'That seems to be a strange arrangement,' she said slowly. 'But not entirely unexpected. It's a male world, huh?'

'You'd better believe it.'

'So tell me, Mr Quinn. If you *were* married, and you *did* arrange a meeting, what would your wife have to do?'

'Like everywhere,' he grumbled, 'there's a lot of protocol. My wife would have to appear with me when we arrive. Then she would be introduced to the women's council. I don't know what goes on inside that outfit. Nobody is willing to say a word about it. Ceremonies, I suppose. Tea and crumpets, for all I know.'

'I don't suppose they'd want to check your marriage licence, or anything like that?'

'Of course not,' he sighed. 'I told you about the bush telegraph. Those people know everything that goes on in our camp. So if I turned up at Topari with a wife, she'd have to be someone they've heard about somewhere.'

'And this is the only way you know that at least one of us could get into that council?'

'It's impossible,' he stated. 'These people aren't fools.'

'Nothing's impossible,' Mattie insisted. 'It's important to the company—very important. So we shall produce a wife for you, and the pair of you will be off for—where did you say?'

'Topari,' he repeated. 'What sort of pipe-dream are you having now?'

'Not a pipe-dream,' she told him solemnly. 'All we need is a Caucasian woman, relatively young, to play the part of wife for you.'

'And where might we find one?' he asked. 'Say a few magic phrases? Pluck one out of mid-air?'

'Don't be so unobservant,' she snapped at him. 'Here I am!'

Ryan turned carefully, his jaw falling open. 'You?' he spluttered. 'You'd be my wife? Good lord, I'd rather wrestle a crocodile!'

Mattie sniffed indignantly. 'I'd probably prefer that myself. But for the company I'm willing to do—almost—anything!'

Ryan threw back his head and laughed. It was the first time she had really seen him enjoy himself. He laughed so hard that tears came to his eyes. And when he recovered and looked at her he was grinning—the same sort of grin the wolf wore as he waited in the forest for Little Red Riding Hood.

'I said—almost,' she repeated sternly. 'I realise that if we're to appear as a twosome we'll have to make use of your bush telegraph. Sort of, while we're in camp, appear more——'

'Loving?' he proposed.

'Well—outwardly,' she agreed primly.

'A little outward hugging?' he suggested, his grin growing wider.

'In public,' she agreed. 'Nothing more.'

'I hardly think it would be believable without a little kissing,' he offered, and she lifted her head and glanced sharply at him. If there was laughter in his eyes she couldn't find it.

'Well—I suppose so. But only in public, on widely separate occasions, and with no fancy business in between! Will that do it?'

'It's hardly going to work,' he announced. 'We're talking about man-and-wifing it, not a casual summer engagement.'

'So?'

'Nobody is going to swallow the bait as long as you're living in the women's quarters, and I'm all alone in my bungalow!'

'Hey, wait just a minute!' protested Mattie. 'That's carrying things pretty far down the pike!'

'The only way,' he said softly. Mattie moved restlessly away and then came back.

'You know, I wouldn't consider this at all if it weren't for the company's need,' she repeated.

'Of course. I understand that entirely.'

'Then why do I have this mad thought that I'm being manipulated?'

'It was all your idea, lady. I *told* you it isn't possible for us to do anything. I still believe that.'

'Damn you,' she moaned. 'All right, go ahead. Send the word. Get us some kind of appointment—for Mr Quinn and his wife. And remember—if you put one foot false, I'll have you singing soprano for the rest of your life!'

'Hey, it's all your idea,' he protested. 'When will you move in?'

Mattie shook her head disgustedly. 'There's no use postponing bad medicine. I'll do it tonight. But what I would like to know, Mr Quinn, is why, all of sudden, you're so willing to co-operate. How about a little truth on *that* subject?'

'So I'll tell you,' he muttered. 'It's obvious that you don't like me. When this thing is over, I don't want a woman hanging on my arm looking for something more. I reckon I have a better chance with you than with some simpleton who dreams fancy dreams.'

Mattie had expected some strong statement, but this was like being kicked in the stomach by a Missouri mule. I'll get you for this, Ryan Quinn, she threatened under her breath. Nobody makes a cipher out of Mattie Latimore!

'Well?' he prodded angrily.

'You're darn right.' She scowled at him so he could read the message in stereo. 'I can't imagine why any reasonable woman would want to marry you, Mr Quinn.'

'Which you aren't,' he muttered before she could catch her breath. 'Reasonable, I mean.'

Slow down, she warned herself. This one has a massive ego. He deserves to be punctured, but it will take a little planning. And her logical engineering mind began to scheme.

'OK, then, that's what we'll do,' she said pleasantly. 'But there is a problem that arises.' A grin flashed across his face. He looked like the kid who had won second prize in a skateboard contest and found out it was a week's worth of chocolate éclairs.

'The problem is,' Mattie said primly, 'that you have to figure some way to keep Virginia from murdering me while this play is running!'

CHAPTER FOUR

It was one thing to laugh about it on an isolated hilltop, and tease Ryan at will, but another entirely to carry on the scheme in the heart of a settled construction camp, Mattie told herself wearily. They had driven back from their expedition in a happy mood. She was openly flirting with him; he was taking it all with a grain of salt, but smiling just the same. When they came through the gate, the tall Nuer guard waved them a friendly welcome, but when they drew up in front of the guest bungalow it was a different story entirely.

Ahmed bin Raschid was standing stiffly on the front porch, and Virginia was in the open doorway.

'Just walk in and start packing,' Ryan advised.

'In case you haven't noticed,' Mattie hissed, 'the lions up there are outside their cages and look like they want to bite. Why should I want to commit suicide?'

'All it takes is a little courage,' he said, giving her a small push between the shoulderblades as she stumbled up the stairs.

'*Ya bint,*' sneered Ahmed, in slow and classic Arabic, 'I think I must check your papers again. You will come with me.' He grabbed for her arm, but very suddenly Ryan was between them.

'If you want to check her papers, you do it here,' he said in the same language. They both spoke slowly enough so that Mattie could make the translations for herself. But there was a very ominous tone in Ryan's voice that would have been plain no matter what language he used. 'Miss Latimore is the vice-president of this organisation, and everything will be done in a very cordial manner, my friend. You will not forget that I have a direct radio contact with the president of police in Khartoum, and with all the international media.'

Ahmed's face turned from olive to purple. 'You forget that I am the government authority in Kosti!' he raged.

'*You* forget that you're standing in the middle of a Latimore camp,' Ryan returned. 'Our guards are not too friendly with government authority. You could have an accident, Ahmed, and none of us want that, do we?'

'Why do you interfere?' the Sudanese growled.

'Because the young lady has come under my cloak,' Ryan said evenly, and emphasised the situation by putting his arm around her shoulders. Mattie shivered. *Under my cloak* had a specific meaning among the desert tribes.

'There'll be another time,' Ahmed snarled as he thumped down the stairs. He hesitated as Ryan said, still in Arabic, just slowly enough for Mattie to translate, 'If there is, Ahmed, there will be mourning among your father's tents.' The official turned pale and then stomped away.

'*Inshallah,*' Ryan reflected at his disappearing back. 'If God wills it.'

'What was all that gibberish about?' Virginia asked shrilly. The former Mrs Quinn was in a violent temper; her voice and face reflected it. Mattie winced.

'Nothing important,' said Ryan. 'Get about it, Mattie.' Both women went into the house. Mattie pulled down her bags and began throwing things into them, helter-skelter, while Virginia sat down on her bed, nervously puffing at a cigarette, glaring.

'Do I take it you're leaving?'

'Not exactly.' Mattie stopped to look at her. There was a calculating look in the woman's eye, and a little smirk of satisfaction playing around her tight lips. She's not

unbalanced, Mattie thought, she's sick. She's wearing a
sleek, svelte shape, but look at her eyes, all bloodshot
and haggard! The woman ought to be in hospital, not
in the middle of the Sudan. Something should be done
about it!

'Virginia,' she said, 'I have a little money of my own
with me. You don't look well enough to be here in Africa.
I could get you a flight back home?'

'Back home? You must be out of your mind!' raged
Virginia. 'If I put one foot in the United States without
seventeen thousand dollars, I'm dead, damn you!'

Mathilda Latimore had grown up poor in a rich family.
Her father had assigned all the children a good al-
lowance; her mother had required strict accounting of
every penny spent. Every child was required to work—
either at home or in some outside job—and none of them
had ever resented it. Still, seventeen thousand dollars
was a great deal of money. Mattie sank back into a chair,
mouth ajar.

'Seventeen thousand?' she gasped.

'Seventeen thousand.' Virginia dropped her cigarette
to the floor and ground it into the linoleum.

'Where could anybody get seventeen thousand dollars
in a hurry?' Mattie asked in awe.

'Ryan has a ranch in Texas,' Virginia grated, 'worth
ten times that much. I'm sure he'll sell it—eventually.
He thinks a lot of me. But you're not doing me any
good. Ryan is my insurance, and I don't intend to let
you cancel the policy! You're leaving the Sudan?'

'No, not exactly.' Mattie jumped to her feet and
managed to close two of her bags. The other bulged
beyond its capacity to close.

'So what exactly is it that you're up to?' Virginia
insisted.

'I'm—just moving to another building. There's not enough room here to spread out. You know.'

'Of course,' Virginia said bitterly. 'Not enough for a vice-president, of course. How did you get that title—by going to bed with the president?'

Mattie stopped. For two cents she would love to tear each tiny little brunette hair off the woman's head, sick or not! Ryan thinks a lot of Virginia, she thought. Now, why should that bother me?

'No, I never slept with the president,' she answered coldly. 'But my mother did,' she added.

'Well, I——' Virginia started to say, when Ryan thundered on the door, and without waiting for an invitation, came in.

'Aren't you ready yet?' he grumbled in his most surly voice.

'My case won't close,' Mattie explained belligerently. And now all three of us are mad, she thought. I wonder which one will blow up first?

'Here, move over,' he ordered. One muscled arm pushed, the other fastened, and the suitcase responded like any well-trained container should. Ryan looked around the room. 'This everything?'

'Yes. Everything but me,' Mattie returned. Swallowing her anger, she tried to appear meek and mild, but almost any observer could have seen through her disguise.

'Then let's go.' Ryan swung all three cases up and stalked out. Mattie shrugged her shoulders and followed, turning back at the door.

'I'm sure we'll see more of each other,' she called back. 'Unless you plan to leave very soon?'

'I plan to leave as soon as I get the deed to that ranch,' the other woman snapped. 'And just *where* are you moving?'

'I don't know,' Mattie answered. 'Wherever Ryan says, I suppose.' Out of the corner of her eye, she could see Virginia reach for a hairbrush on top of the bureau. She didn't look as if she were about to brush her hair. Experienced by being raised in a house full of volatile sisters, Mattie ducked out of the door and closed it behind her. By the time she heard the dull thud and saw the door rocking from the impact, she was already crawling into the jeep.

Ryan's bungalow was just across from the administration building, and appeared to be twice as big as the guest cottage. Mattie crawled warily out of the car. There was no way for a woman to get out of an old jeep gracefully, and this one, like those on most big construction jobs, was a military re-tread. A little brushing restored law and order to Mattie's clothing, and by that time Ryan had come around the vehicle to her side.

'This is a good time for it,' he announced. Mattie looked up cautiously.

'A good time for what?'

'That hugging and kissing bit,' he said blithely. 'There's an audience across the street.'

'Oh, boy,' she muttered. 'If this wasn't for the good of the corporation—who the devil is going to explain all this to my mother?'

'Mother?' he laughed. 'That little lady back in Boston? Your father I could worry about, but that little lady?'

'That's the one,' Mattie returned mournfully. 'Mary-Kate believes in the old Teddy Roosevelt dictum: walk softly, and carry a big stick. And we'd better drum up a good explanation, or she'll hand you your head before you get past the front door!'

'I'd practise ducking,' he countered. 'But I don't expect to go by the Boston area any time soon. Come on, girl, pucker up!'

That's something else I seem to have forgotten, Mattie sighed to herself as she complied. He *won't* be going back to Boston with me—thank God. She might have reasoned it all out, given a few more seconds, but the kissing suddenly required all her attention, and the whole conversation slipped her mind.

Inside the house, still having trouble with her breathing, she waited for Ryan to bring in the luggage, peering out through the curtained windows to watch. Item number one: curtains on the windows. She looked around hastily. Carpets on the floor. Heavy, comfortable furniture. An air-conditioner talking to itself in the corner window. An open bathroom door, complete with tub and shower and mirror. And three closed doors. She had her hand on the knob of the first one when Ryan tramped in and sat her bags down with a thud.

'Turn the damn air-conditioner up,' he ordered as he wiped his forehead with his neckcloth. Mattie sauntered over in that direction, examined the front panel, and turned the right knob. 'Don't know why it got so hot so suddenly,' he grumbled.

'Me neither,' she chuckled, then burst out laughing. He stared at her as if she had suddenly taken leave of her senses.

'I suppose that's some sort of New England joke,' he said. 'It went completely over my head. That's your room, the one on the end. The middle door is the kitchen.' He picked up her bags again and followed her across to the closed door. Mattie looked up at him pertly as she opened it and went in.

'I don't believe I ever met a man with less sense of humour than you,' she sighed.

'No, I don't suppose you have,' he returned solemnly.
He dropped the bags in one corner, started for the door,
then changed his mind. 'And that's a funny thing,' he
added, 'because people tell me I was the happiest kid in
the world when I was young. Want a drink?'

She followed him this time, out to the central room.
He disappeared into the kitchen and came back in a
moment with two glasses. Mattie settled back into one
of the padded chairs and accepted the offering. Ryan
leaned one hip on the table for a moment, then moved
to the chair beside her and raised his glass, toasting her.

Mattie took one sip and knew that her throat was going
to be burned to cinders. It was not the ladylike thing to
do, but she managed to spit it all out. 'What in God's
name——' she rasped. Ryan was back from the kitchen
again, with water, which he force-fed her. She coughed
madly, and he pounded on her back.

'All right, all right,' she moaned. 'You didn't poison
me, so there's no need to beat me to death!'

'I certainly didn't mean to do either one,' he said. 'My
God, I wouldn't——'

Mattie waited in anticipation to find out what he
'wouldn't——' but he never finished the sentence.

Her racking cough under control, she wiped her eyes
and leaned back in the chair, almost able to breathe.
'What was that?' she repeated.

'*Rakki,*' he said. 'Nothing but a simple double-distilled
palm wine. All the natives drink it.'

'No wonder they're not affected by the local diseases,'
she sighed. 'What bug would *dare* to infect them with
that in their blood?'

'You're better?' As soon as she nodded, Ryan's face
turned to stone again.

'I'm only a beer drinker,' she explained, 'and not much
of that.'

'We have Kaffir beer,' he returned, 'but it's thirty per cent alcohol, and I thought that might be too strong for you.'

'Thank you for your concern,' she muttered. 'I don't suppose you have any lemonade?'

'Not a chance.' And this time she definitely caught the little twitch at the right corner of his mouth. 'Anything you drink that's made with water has to be boiled. Tea is the magic word. May I fetch you a cup of tea?'

'I don't believe it,' she groaned. 'OK, a cup of tea. No cream, no sugar.' Again that little suggestion of a smile as he looked down at her, then walked back into the kitchen. She watched him move away. Again that smooth acceleration, that gliding, tiger-like motion. There was a word she needed, and she fumbled for it. Alert, that was it. He walked alertly, as if sampling everything around him at all times.

I've spent too much of my young life studying engineering, haven't I? she thought. It wasn't a question, but one followed. What have I missed? Before an answer could develop Ryan was back, with a steaming mug of tea in his hands. The silence weighed on Mattie's brain. He sipped at his glass as though the drink was well-water, while she struggled to cool the tea without burning herself. And they watched each other across the few feet that separated them.

'A very fancy place,' she essayed, trying to break the silence. 'Pretty posh.'

'Rank has its privileges,' he returned. And the silence overwhelmed them again.

'Your wife——' Mattie started to say.

'My former wife,' Ryan interrupted. But at least he moved, spoke, looked interested, so Mattie took another step forward.

'She looks ill,' she offered.

'Now what?' he asked, but there was no bitterness in the voice. 'You want my life history?'

'Not exactly.' Don't let him think you're too interested, girl!

'OK, I'll tell you about my wife,' he declared, and again that little twitch was present at the corner of his mouth. 'Virginia and I were married eight years ago. It was a dynastic marriage. She wanted it, my mother and father wanted it, and I didn't care. It didn't work out. I divorced her six years ago.'

'Six years is a long time,' Mattie said sympathetically. 'Did you never ever meet another woman you might want to marry?'

'I've met one or two,' he acknowledged, 'but marriage is out. I'm going to have Virginia hanging around my neck like an albatross for the rest of our lives.'

'You feel *that* responsible for her?' Mattie felt a little pinpoint of pain in her heart. It wasn't sympathy—not by any means—but she wasn't sure just what name to put to it.

'Of course I'm responsible for her,' he muttered. 'Eight years ago we were a trio—Joe Sullivan, Virginia, and I. She married me, and it took her a year to realise she'd chosen the wrong guy. Virginia left me and moved in with Joe, and two years later he went bankrupt and committed suicide. He was from one of the richest families in Texas, and he went bankrupt. Can you imagine that?'

'I—suppose so,' Mattie returned sympathetically. 'Texas and oil go hand in hand. I understand that times are exceedingly tough in Texas right now. So that broke Virginia up, I suppose?'

'Yes, it broke her up,' he answered. 'Not Joe's death—and he wasn't in oil at all—it was the bankruptcy. She spent him into it. In case you hadn't noticed, my former wife is a compulsive gambler!'

'I thought that was a sort of joke people made up,' Mattie stammered.

'Joke, hell,' muttered Ryan, refilling his glass. 'It's a real disease.'

'She says——' Mattie hesitated, considering her own audacity, but she wanted to know. It was important for her to know, even though she had no logical reason. 'She said she needed—a great deal of money.'

'She surely does,' he agreed bitterly. 'She took out a loan. I'm going to let her sweat for a while.'

'But I'm sure the bank could rearrange the payments,' Mattie suggested.

Ryan gulped down his second full glass of poison. 'For a vice-president, you're a naïve little girl,' he said gruffly. 'The bank she's dealing with has this way of collecting on their loans. They break kneecaps. Surely you don't think she came all the way to the Sudan about a simple bank loan?'

That's something you only hear in television stories, Mattie thought frantically. Strictly fiction! But she had the tiniest doubt. 'You *are* going to help her?'

'Of course I am,' he sighed. 'I'm the cause of most of her problems, so I'm going to help her—eventually. And then she'll go along for a year or two, and fall down again, and I'm going to help her again—and again. Until one or both of us falls over dead. *Now* do you understand?'

'It isn't too important to me,' she said carefully. 'When are we going to go up-country?'

Ryan gave her a disgusted look. 'I started the arrangements hours ago,' he drawled. 'We should be hearing very soon. In the meantime, don't go outside this camp. Ahmed isn't noted for his forgiveness.'

'You make this whole country sound terrible!' she shouted at him. 'It can't be all *that* bad! Ahmed is just a little boy whose position is going to his head!'

'It's *not* that bad,' he growled. 'I told you before—it never was really a country—the present Moslem government is trying to *make* it a country the best way they know how. The rebels are trying to take away a part and make it a *separate* country, and I can't blame them for that. And the tribes are trying to keep their own governments and customs, and I can't blame them for *that*, either. As for Ahmed, he's a big frog in a little puddle. In a land racked by rebellion there are bound to be a few like him. But don't get the idea that he's a foolish little boy. He's mean, he's powerful in this area, and he's vindictive.' He glared at her, then marched over to the door. 'I'm going across the street to check on things. I'll send your supper over from the canteen.'

Mattie stared at his back as he walked away, wondering just where knives could be placed to provide the most torture. 'Ahmed is mean and vindictive?' she muttered. 'Lord, that kid's in good company!'

Supper arrived as predicted, delivered by a string of Masakin Qisar, the so-called 'short Nuba', who matched Northern European standards of height, and lived in villages interspersed between the Masakin Tiwal, the giant Nuba who averaged over six feet tall. The men set up a table with spartan efficiency, then stood patiently by until Ryan arrived. After a brief inspection of the table, he waved a hand and they disappeared.

'I didn't expect you to dinner,' Mattie commented as her bright blue eyes scanned his neat new appearance. Even a shirt and tie, she noted. Score one for the mighty hunter? She had used the hours to bathe luxuriously, making maximum use of all the perks she had criticised him for having. Her hair, newly washed and combed, sparkled in the light, falling gently to her shoulders, making a showcase of her clear complexion, her slightly darker eyebrows, her beautiful teeth. With assurance that the air-conditioners were doing their job, she wore her only formal dress, a three-quarter-length amber silk with a bodice cut deeply between her breasts, and clinging lovingly at her hips. Apart from one quick inspection, she noticed, Ryan gave her about as much attention as he did the platter of veal that was the centrepiece.

'I didn't think I would, either,' he admitted, 'but I managed to clean up all the work in no time. Besides, this is the ideal time to put on our show. Half those men are leaving in the morning, going home to their tribes. Nice.' He ran his tongue around the words as if savouring them.

'Yeah, nice,' Mattie returned. 'Spread the word—Ryan bin Quinn visits his *harem*! I'm going to write a book about this when I get home.'

'If you do, I'll break your neck,' he threatened ominously. 'Publicity I don't need—not in the US of A.'

'Hah!' she snorted. 'You won't be close enough to find out!'

'Don't be too sure of that,' he said, but his heart wasn't in it. He was remembering what *he* had said to *her* not too long ago. 'Well, we shouldn't be fighting *all* the time.' He helped her to her chair and took the one opposite, lifting the covers of the hot dishes one at a time. 'Not too bad. Rice, veal, lentils. May I serve you?'

It would be graceless to carry on like this for ever, Mattie's conscience told her. Ma would raise a fuss if she ever found out. Politeness—that was her major directive. So Mattie Latimore dug deeply for her most polite smile, and acquiesced.

They ate in leisurely fashion, sharing a bottle of
Moroccan wine with the meal, and making small talk.
When the food was gone, Mattie cleared away the dishes,
stacking them on a coffee table by the door, and the two
of them nursed their drinks.

'Any word about our trip?' she asked.

Ryan nodded over his glass. 'Plenty—more words than
I'd care to hear. We'll leave the day after tomorrow, after
midnight.'

'That soon?' she gasped. 'I thought I'd get a chance
to use one of those nice soft beds for a few nights! Why
the hurry?'

'First,' he said, dabbing at his mouth with a napkin,
'the *Sanda*, the festival, starts soon, and all the tribes
will be gathering at Topari. It's just the right time for
us to show up.'

'That makes sense,' she admitted. 'But why not in
three or four days? I'm a girl who needs her eight hours'
sleep more regularly. You said *first*. Am I to understand
there's a *second* involved here someplace?'

'I guess you might say so,' he drawled. She had never
heard him sound more Texan than he did at that
moment. 'Ahmed has put a guard on our gate. They
have instructions, so I'm told, to watch for the gold-
haired *ferenqi*.'

'Oh, my!' Her stomach made a little unexpected jump.
'I—don't suppose you have any other blonde foreigners
working here?'

'Nobody but you,' he chuckled.

'My God,' she exclaimed, 'is *that* the sort of thing
you think is funny? That mad Sudanese is waiting out
there to cut me up in little pieces? That's funny?'

'Hey, don't go into hysterics,' he rumbled. 'I really
don't think he has anything more on his mind than
seduction.'

He got up and came around the table, offering his arms for comfort. She needed some—comfort, that was—and his was the best offer. Otherwise I'd never come near the man, she told herself as she was pressed gently against his chest. But only for a minute. If there was anything the Latimore girls all had besides beauty, it was pride, and Mattie's surfaced quickly as she pushed away from him. His arms opened instantly as she stepped back a pace or two and fell on to the sofa behind her.

'No, I guess it wasn't all that funny,' he mused, watching her carefully. 'Maybe I need lessons on humour?'

'I could get some cue cards,' she offered, her equanimity restored. 'How am I going to get out of here if Ahmed has the gates under guard?'

'Modern technology,' Ryan said pompously. 'Helicopter.'

'You mean to tell me I took that crazy boat ride for nothing? You had a helicopter all the time? Why, you——' And her tongue failed her again.

'I don't mean to tell you anything!' he shouted back. With her blue eyes glaring, her cheeks pink, her breasts swelling with rage, her tiny fists clenched prepared for an assault, she had suddenly become the most desirable woman he had ever seen. His own emotions shocked him, and he hurried to qualify his statement.

'It's more complicated than just not telling you,' he sighed. 'We have two helicopters. Ordinarily we use them everywhere, but in the last three weeks the rebels have sent raiding parties up as far as the Kordofan. And they have some sort of anti-aircraft rockets. So we've grounded the choppers.'

'So, to avoid Ahmed's company, I get to be a flying target?' Mattie asked bitterly.

'My God,' he roared, 'can't I ever get on the right track with you? Every time I bring up something you find fault. No, you won't be a flying target. The rebels are not much at night-fighting. We'll use the choppers to lift us out of Ahmed's territory, then we'll switch to land transport.'

Not having anything else to find fault with, she fell back on sophism. 'Don't yell at me,' she muttered. 'I'm not some new little kid on the block!'

'I'll yell if I please!' roared Ryan. And then, softly, 'Oh, hell! Very well, I won't yell at you.' For a few seconds they glared at each other. 'How about some coffee?' he offered as a peace-offering. Mattie managed a little smile and returned to the table.

For a full five minutes they managed to talk without arguing. The weather, her schooling as a member of one of the elite families of Massachusetts, his anecdotes about growing up as the only son on a cattle ranch. Mattie was beginning to feel quite proud of herself, when the peace was shattered. Virginia Quinn threw back the door, stalked in, and slammed it behind her.

'So this is what you're up to!' she shrilled at them both. 'I knew there was something going on between you two! Having a little *private* dinner, are you, before you get to bed? I told you, Blondie, not to fool around!'

'I'm not fooling around,' Mattie returned stoutly, without giving thought to the double meaning. It was another Latimore attribute—never back down in the face of physical abuse. 'And if I were, I fail to see that it's any business of yours!'

'I'm going to make it my business!' Virginia snarled.

'You've had too much to drink,' Ryan interjected as he got up slowly from his chair. 'Calm down, Virginia. We're only planning company strategy.'

'Sure you are,' his former wife sneered. 'I can see it all clearly. She puts on one of those vanishing-front see-through dresses so she can talk business. Do you take me for a country girl?'

'You don't seem to get the picture,' Ryan grated. 'I've told you before—I don't take you *at all*!'

'I don't have to stand for this!' the woman screamed. 'Somebody's going to suffer!' For that brief second they were all poised as in a tableau; the sinking feeling struck Mattie that the 'somebody' who was going to suffer was bound to be herself.

Virginia Quinn confirmed it. With another scream, she dived across the dinner table at Mattie, scattering dishes and coffee-pot alike. Both her hands were raised and spread, her red-painted nails pointing like ten little daggers at Mattie's face.

Luckily, Mattie's reflexes were as sharp as her tongue, and both her hands came up protectively. At the same time, she pushed back against her chair, sending it straight back and down.

Ryan was no slow starter himself. Virginia had come in wearing a blouse and slacks. Before she could think of her next manoeuvre, he had grasped her, one hand on the collar of her blouse, the other in the waistband of her slacks. He lifted her up, still struggling, and walked around the table with her to the door, where he lowered her to her feet.

The fight had gone out of her. When Ryan whispered a few words into her ear she started to cry, then walked out of the door as he opened it. He stood in the doorway for a moment, then gently closed the door again.

Mattie set her chair back up, looked at the mess on and around the coffee table, and bent to pick up the nearest piece of debris.

'Leave it,' commanded Ryan. 'A couple of the cleaners will get it in the morning.'

'Yeah, sure,' Mattie sighed, straightening up. 'I must say it's—interesting—to meet your friends, Mr Quinn. What did you tell her that made her walk out of here?'

'What else? I told her I'd break her fool neck for her if she didn't cut it out instantly!'

'I might have known,' Mattie muttered. 'Always the macho answer!' She put her hands on her hips and looked around. 'Well, if I have to pack and leave, I'd better start. How long will we be gone?'

'Ten to fifteen days,' he said. 'Bring your travel stuff—and a couple of those *dishdashes* that you bought in Kosti.'

'Typical male answer!' she snapped in disgust. 'You said something about my seeing the queen. I suppose there'll be ceremonies?'

'Of course,' he allowed. 'While I talk to the council, you talk to the queen.'

'So tell me, oh, fount of wisdom,' she asked sarcastically, 'I'll want to fit in with the company. What will the women be wearing for these functions?'

This time it was the biggest grin she had ever seen anywhere. 'Well now, I hadn't thought of that,' chuckled Ryan. 'Interesting. I suppose it would be proper for you to blend in with the ladies.'

'So what will they be wearing?' she snapped. That grin on his face spread, if such a thing were possible.

'Nothing,' he said blandly. 'The Masakin believe in ceremonial nakedness.'

CHAPTER FIVE

'WELL, I'll say this much for you,' Mattie said sarcastically. 'You're an arrogant son-of-a-gun. Where's the helicopter?'

'It'll come,' shrugged Ryan. 'It wouldn't dare *not* come. I told the pilot you were the passenger and he was instantly petrified.'

She glared daggers at him. They were squatting on the ground just outside the camp's marked helicopter pad, in total darkness. The night wind was chilling. Nothing stirred. At the other end of the camp the main gates were closed. A squad of six Sudanese soldiers stood outside, a platoon of twenty Nuer warriors stood inside. And it was all *his* fault.

'I imagine you must consider yourself a self-made man,' she snapped querulously.

'Of course. What else? What's all this leading up to?' he asked cautiously.

'It restores my faith,' she commented. 'Being self-made, you relieve God of the blame for a terrible mistake!'

There was silence for a moment. The tip of Ryan's pipe glowed as he inhaled. 'Now that,' he said drily, 'that's funny!'

'Yes—well,' she stuttered, fishing for a smart remark and finding none. Instead, she came up with a *non sequitur*: 'I'm getting cold.'

'Hey,' Ryan said softly, moving closer to her side, 'I know you don't like me, but it would help the mission if you would *not like me* less intensely.'

Mattie's innate honesty was stung. 'I don't mean to let personalities mix with business,' she apologised. 'I've been looking around a little. I admire your administrative skill, your leadership qualities——'

'But personally?'

'Well——' She shrugged her shoulders in the dark. There was no sense lying about it. 'Personally—you're right. I just don't like you. I'm sorry, but there it is.'

'Yes—and here it is,' muttered Ryan, pulling her back from the circle-marked landing pad. The distant speck of sound turned into a roar, landing lights flashed above their heads, and were instantly matched by the floodlights illuminating the landing pad. The tired old chopper settled down on its fan of dust and shook itself to a stop.

'It could stand a paint job!' she snapped at him.

'Now that's what I mean,' he returned. 'Isn't there *anything* that you don't criticise? Yes, it needs paint; more than that, it needs a new motor—and come to think of it, the pilot needs a rest, too! What else do you have to say?'

The side door of the helicopter slid back and a small ladder slid out. 'If it's paint you need, requisition it,' Mattie shouted at Ryan over her shoulder. 'If it's a relief pilot, I'd be glad to take over.'

He neglected the ladder, boosting her up into the passenger compartment as if she were a pound of feathers, and vaulting up beside her. 'Now you're a pilot?' he said, disbelieving.

'Since I was seventeen years old.'

'Oh, since last week?'

She started to answer, but quickly discovered he had outplayed her. She had no intention of telling him her true age. Not that twenty-five was old, she reasoned, but just because it was none of his business. He was strapping himself into a seat on the opposite side of the

cabin; she glared at him, but there was no sensible thing
for her to do except follow suit. The interior lights went
out before she could think of anything else. The big machine rattled, roared, and stumbled into the air. The
landing lights went out instantly. They turned in a slight
bank and headed west.

It was almost impossible to communicate with Ryan.
There was no amplifier-telephone system available, and
the noise inside the craft was twice as high as outside.
She tried twice to shout above the clatter, but to no avail.
He added insult to injury by leaning across the aisle and
passing her a pair of plastic and rubber earplugs.

I *like* the quiet, she told herself dismally. It was a real
lie—Mattie Latimore loved to talk to people. All sizes,
all kinds, she loved to talk. And occasionally listen. Not
too often that—listening was her sister Becky's trait. The
aircraft bucked and banged, keeping low against the
land, following the double track, road and railroad, that
ran side by side towards the mountains of Darfur. Her
thoughts wandered as she watched him. He had instantly buried himself in papers, working steadily in the
weak light of the chopper's cabin. Here they were, em-
barked on an adventure that might save the company's
life in Middle Africa, and he was up to his nose in
paperwork!

He needed a haircut, she judged. Well, at least a trim.
Dressed for travel, in jeans and dark shirt, his bush hat
lying on the floor beside him, Ryan Quinn was still the
epitome of neatness, glowing with health. But a tiny
fringe of brown hair ran down to the nape of his neck.
I'll bet a million women have run their fingers through
that mop, she thought, then laughed at herself. There
had been a young fellow student at MIT with an en-
trancing head of hair. Only when she tried to run her

fingers through it, it turned out to be a hairpiece, and he had never spoken to her again!

Ryan must have caught her thought, for he lowered the paper he was working on and showed her a tiny wisp of a smile before lowering his head again.

'Oh, well,' she muttered, and composed herself to snatch a few minutes' sleep. As it happened, she was unable to shut him out. His face, that little smile, were both inscribed on the insides of her eyelids, haunting her. She hadn't expected that. Over the few years since she had actively worked in the leadership of the corporation, she had learned to put up a cool but determined front.

'You have a double burden,' her father had told her once. 'I know you're a good engineer—one of the best— but to most of our men you'll be the boss's daughter. It's only by proving *how* good an engineer you are that you'll get over the hump of being a relative of mine. And you'll do it on your own, Mattie. I won't lower the standards, change the orders one iota just because you're my daughter.'

'But off duty you'll still love me?' she had offered pertly, and set about doing just what he had ordered. Successfully. She had worked at half a dozen major projects, discovering that she could give orders as soon as she learned to take orders. Discovering, too, that there was many a soft heart beating under a hard hat. But not with this man. Ryan Quinn was carved out of rock. And with that thought she dropped off to sleep.

It was the landing noises that woke her. The pitch of the giant blades over their heads changed, the machine hovered and rattled all the more, then the undercarriage slammed into the ground. The cabin lights were off; as Mattie peered out of the inconvenient windows she could see nothing. The pilot had landed in total darkness, feeling for the earth with the seat of his pants. She ignored Ryan's proffered hand and clambered out.

They had landed on a little square of savannah grass, about half a mile from hills looming to the south. As her eyes became accustomed to the darkness she saw the dim outline of a vehicle of some sort about twenty yards away. Ryan urged her in that direction. A man passed them, going in the other direction.

'*Hujambo,*' he grunted, and Ryan repeated the greeting.

'Where are we?' asked Mattie in a conspiratorial whisper.

'You can speak up,' he chuckled. 'There's nobody within ten miles in any direction—I hope.'

'But I thought we were flying to Topari?' she queried. 'I don't see any villages around here.'

'Come on,' he urged. 'These are unsettled times, and I don't want to hang around here any longer than we have to. Climb into the Land Rover.' Just to make sure she complied, he added a good push that sent her sprawling over the step and into the vehicle. Mattie was still spluttering when he came around and climbed into the wrong side of the truck. At the same moment the pilot of the helicopter gunned his engines and pulled the old bird back up into the sky.

She shivered. It was more than an hour before dawn, but it wasn't the cool breeze that affected her; it was the sudden thought that they were all alone. Ryan was checking out the load in the vehicle with a little penlight when the thought hit her.

'It's going away,' she said dolefully. He raised his head and stared at her. 'The helicopter,' she added.

'Of course. That's the purpose of the whole affair.'

'Maybe you'd better explain, then. I—don't see a living thing anywhere around but us.'

'Amen,' he remarked sarcastically. 'What's the matter? Cold feet?'

'Aren't I entitled once in a while?' she asked spiritedly.

He leaned across the console of the truck and patted her hand. 'Everybody's entitled. I've had one or two times of sheer panic myself. But I thought the Imperial Miss Latimore—oh, hell, there I go again!' He pulled her over, closer. 'It's nothing to be alarmed about,' he explained. 'We didn't want to take any chances on rebels being in the area, and we wanted to lay a false scent for Ahmed bin Raschid. We're about ten miles from Er Rahad, a fairly safe area of the world. The helicopter is now headed in the opposite direction, for Sennar, on the Blue Nile. They'll be there at dawn, and the bush tele-graph will have the word in Kosti within minutes. That ought to spike Ahmed's little plot, and leave us a clear road ahead.'

'It's like a Sherlock Holmes story,' Mattie laughed, suddenly relieved. 'Everything is so simple once it's ex-plained! I don't know that I like that phrase, though—Ahmed's little plot. Do you actually think he's got something planned?'

'Don't take all this too lightly, Mattie. He's a danger-ous young man, and we're in a part of the world where the law sometimes doesn't run.'

'I won't,' she sighed. 'Thank you.' Ryan increased the pressure on her hand for a moment, then let her go. The car's engine spun into sound, softly muted in the great emptiness around them. Which brought up half a dozen other questions, including, 'How come the inside of this thing is arranged backwards?'

'What?' They were moving without headlights across a flat prairie, and Ryan was leaning forwards over the wheel in order to see. The moon was not helping. It had risen, and immediately ducked behind clouds. 'Oh. You mean the steering wheel? This is a British export model, one of the finest safari trucks in the world. Four-wheel drive, high off the road for bush clearance, dependable engine. Where's that road?'

'Road? We're looking for a road?'

'Not any more,' he chuckled. The vehicle bounced over something that put all its wheels in the air and then came down with a mighty bounce, slewed a little, and resumed its quiet trip. 'We're going south-west now,' he said as he flicked on the headlights. 'Koalib Mountain is about eighty miles ahead of us, cross country.'

The information gave her some sense of security. Mattie had no idea where Koalib Mountain was, but just by having a name it established itself in her mind with permanence. In any event, they did not quite make it to the place. About a mile outside the next village Ryan stopped and pulled off the road about fifty yards.

'This ought to be a good place,' he announced as he shut off the engine. Good place for what? was the message that flashed through her mind. He was on the same frequency.

'We'll camp here for a time and doss down,' he explained. 'Neither of us got any sleep last night. These roads are dangerous.'

'Don't tell me there's a traffic problem,' she snapped. 'I haven't seen another vehicle for the past hour. And I'm not all that happy about camping out on the ground when we're only a few miles from a town. Surely they have a hotel?'

'Not so you'd notice,' he chuckled. 'The nearest village has roughly four hundred inhabitants, no more. We're on the old caravan trail here. There's an old caravanserai in the town. Lots of camels brought lots of fleas—and a few other insects—and left them in the *serai*. I'd rather have a nice clean camp in the open, myself.'

And I'd rather not spend another night too close to you, Mattie told herself. But—fleas, or Ryan Quinn? She flipped a mental coin, and it came up heads.

'It sounds sensible,' she said coolly, and he looked at her in surprise.

'No arguments?'

'None, but I think we'd be better over there among the trees.' They had been travelling across rolling grassland since dawn. About two hundred yards away was a small knoll, covered with a cluster of acacia trees.

'You don't really mean that, do you?' he asked.

'Of *course* I do. It will get us out of the direct sun.'

'Well, as you keep reminding me, you're the boss.' He fired the engine and trundled the vehicle up the incline. They came to a stop in the middle of the grove of trees, whose roots had found water in the dry riverbed nearby. The knoll was too small to be called a hill, and yet, curving up above the plain, afforded them a wide view.

'Like some parts of Texas,' drawled Ryan. 'You can see miles and miles of nothing but miles and miles. I'll get the tent unpacked.'

'I'll give you a hand.' Mattie climbed out of the truck and took a moment or two to flex her muscles. Her legs were stiff from the rough ride. Her arms were trembling from the caution that drove her. I'll get *the* tent—she had heard Ryan perfectly well. *The* tent. And if he comes up with that double bedroll again I'll—what *will* I do? Her practical mind took over just in time to stamp out hysteria. There's certainly no need for two tents, she assured herself. Surely he wouldn't dream of attacking his boss. And lord knows, he's ugly enough so I won't feel like attacking *him*!

With her help, it took only twenty minutes to set up camp and start a little charcoal fire going. While struggling with the back peg she managed, still bent over, to back into one of the trees.

'I've been stabbed!' she cried as she jumped away, tears running down her face. Ryan came running from the fire, took a quick look, and burst out laughing.

'It's not that funny,' she moaned. 'Something's stuck in my—in me. Get it out! And don't you dare laugh!'

'I won't,' he assured her. 'Turn around.'

'You're still laughing,' she accused him over her shoulder.

'No, not really. This is going to hurt for a second.'

'I—— Good lord!' She whirled around to inspect the sharp thorn between his fingers. 'Where did that come from? Why didn't you warn me?'

'I thought you knew,' he said. She could see the corners of his mouth twitching. 'You insisted on camping under these trees. It's not a bad idea—if you're careful. They're known as thorn trees around these parts.'

Another half-hour was required to re-establish Mattie's good temper. As she stood back from the fire and watched Ryan feed it up to size, honesty required her to admit—at least to herself—that he could have probably done all the camp work in ten minutes *without* her help. He looked up at her chuckle.

'I was just wondering,' she mused. 'It's so quiet. No birds, no animals—it's as if the whole country was deserted.'

'You're just about right,' Ryan commented as he hung a pot of water on the little spit and brought out a general-purpose frying-pan. 'The drought ran for a decade—all over the Sahel. The whole western area of Sudan, Ethiopia, Chad, Central African Republic almost dried up and blew away. I heard that once you could find lion and elephant and ostrich, leopard and giraffe and—oh, the usual run of tropical Africa, not to mention birds. All wiped out by the drought. You like powdered eggs?'

'I'll eat anything—once,' Mattie assured him. He poured a little water into the pan and began stirring in the dried egg powder. 'I hear tell some of the birds are coming back,' he continued, stirring the mixture in the pan. 'Up in Malhal...' he pointed towards the western hills '...they say that the *kiljos* are coming back. That's the African stork. You can see a few vultures about now and then. We've had reports of stray single lions showing—mostly elderly males, driven out of the pride. They're the dangerous ones. Along the Nile, everything is back to normal, but out in the bush times are still hard. Oh, and watch out for the snakes, of course.'

'How can you tell the poisonous ones from the others?'

'There aren't any *others*, lady. Try this while I start the coffee.' He handed her another slab of the way-bread she had first tasted on the *Hurriya*. It seemed like years ago. This piece had been slit open and the hollow centre filled with what might be called scrambled eggs. It tasted like ambrosia. And the tea like nectar. Life isn't half bad, Mattie told herself. Even if I have to put up with Ryan Quinn!

He had set up the tent so that all the sides were rolled up, open to the wind. And some dark spirit must have whispered in his ear during the night. There were two separate sleeping-bags, set about as far apart as they possibly could be. She scrubbed the pan with sand while Ryan moved the Land Rover farther under the trees.

'Wouldn't care to have visitors while we sleep,' he remarked. And having thus completely upset her nerves, he pulled off his boots, unbuckled his belt, and stretched out on one of the sleeping-bags. It wasn't that easy for Mattie. She followed suit, but tossed and turned, unable to find a comfortable position. Twice she got up to dig a rock out from under the sleeping-bag. Never in her life had she seen a land where, under the coarse grass cover that looked so inviting, there was so much hard rock!

Nothing seemed to bother *him*. And the more she realised that, the more angry Mattie became. This whole scheme seemed crazier by the minute! Go along with Ryan Quinn because he can't be heard in the council unless he's married? That's about as thin an excuse as I've ever heard! So why did I fall in with the gag? Because I believed him? It would take a real meathead to fall for *any* line put out by Ryan Quinn! Why? Because *he* didn't put it out—you did, dummy!

Mattie's eyes blinked for a second or two. The sun was rising, burning off the clouds that had threatened from the east. The temperature zoomed upwards, as if the thermometers were about to commit suicide, and her eyes blinked once more.

She was fast asleep, breathing deep in her throat, when Ryan opened an eye, checked the situation, rolled over on his side, and spent a pleasant few minutes watching her. Her blonde hair lay in disarray around her mobile face as she chased some dream. Her hands clenched and unclenched, and both her blouse and camisole had twisted up, exposing the soft, tanned skin of her hip and navel. He couldn't control the smile. All vice-presidents are equal, he grinned to himself, but some are more equal than others. The morning heat began to seep into his mind, and he too fell into sleep. And pursued dreams that hadn't occurred to him in years.

The heat soothed Mattie too, then it went away. She had not bothered to crawl into the sleeping-bag. Instead, from force of circumstance, she had taken off her boots and stretched out on top of the bag. The chill touched her feet, always her most sensitive part, and almost awakened her. Almost, not quite. A dream flashed in front of her closed eyelids. She was running in the dark, trying to escape? No, trying to catch up. But her goal was far ahead of her, moving away, and she was handicapped by mistakes. The earth rocked, as if she were in a boat, constrained by her stupid clothing. A wild hand threatened her with a thorn, and an echoing voice sounded in her ears: 'How can you lead when you can't even follow?' From his mountain top, Thor hurled a thunderbolt at her, and flashes of warfare on each side of her path forced her, trembling, to stay in its middle. And then she fell down into the river, and her face was wet. Mattie woke up, screaming, and scrambled to her knees.

'Now what's the matter?' Ryan was out of his bedroll and at her side as the thunder crashed, enfolding her with his warm, protective arms, sheltering her from the huge raindrops that belted the tent.

The Wet had come.

The two of them knelt together for minutes, holding each other, watching the rain. Ryan was making soothing noises. Mattie was doing her best to establish control over her scattered senses. It took a deal of doing, but she succeeded.

'I'm all right,' she told him. 'I don't understand.'

'You were tired,' he comforted. 'It surprised you. The rainy season has started, but I didn't expect it to begin with a thunderstorm.'

'They told me in Boston,' she sighed. 'It's going to rain for three months?'

'Not as bad as that,' he reassured her. 'In the next three months, there will be rain, yes. I think perhaps something like thirty days' worth. The only problem is that the whole year's rain will come down in that thirty days. Look at the size of those drops, will you!'

Mattie had done nothing but look since she'd woken. The flat surface of the savannah all around them was being beaten into mud flats by the rain, whose drops looked as big as New England hailstones. The whole world sighed. The acacias above them held back the storm for a minute, then the leaves gave way, providing a secondary shower. Lightning flashed in massive sheets to their right and left.

'We've got to get out of here,' Ryan muttered in her ear.

'Get out of here in *that*! You're out of your mind!'

'Hey—you're an engineer,' he shouted at her. 'Where are we? Lightning is striking all around the area, we're in the middle of a flat plain, on top of a hill. What does that tell you, boss-lady?'

Mattie's mind began to work feebly. Flat country, high hill, lightning: it all added up to disaster. She could still remember vividly a scene from her childhood: a soccer practice on a flat field, a coach telling the players to keep working when a thunderstorm rolled by. A lightning strike. Two players and the coach, all dead.

'Where do we run to?' she gasped.

'There's a dry *wadi* over there to our left,' Ryan shouted. 'A ditch, lady. Right after the next bolt, run like hell!'

Mattie fumbled for her boots, then decided to carry them rather than spend the time putting them on. His hand in the middle of her shoulders urged her on. She covered the hundred yards in record speed, keeping low to the ground. The open *wadi*, a depression hardly three feet deep, looked better and better the closer she got. Ryan gave her no time for a dramatic entrance. One strong push sent her flying over the edge in a swan dive, with his weight falling almost on top of her an instant later.

'Keep your head down,' he shouted over the wailing of the storm. 'It won't last long! And get your butt down!'

Mattie hugged the earth as a lover would, straining to get closer. There was only one trouble. The water, having to run off somewhere, had chosen the *wadi* to be that place. Instead of a dry ditch, within minutes they were up to their necks in the stuff. 'No,' cautioned Ryan. 'Keep your nose above water, but don't get up!'

Mattie could see over the edge of the ditch, and the seeing was a scary sight. Not a quarter of a mile from them, lightning had smashed into another grove of trees, and despite the torrents of water falling on their heads, the trees were ablaze.

'You all right?' asked Ryan, crawling up beside her.

'Yes.' She was, she knew. Despite all the carnage around them, she was all right. Safe in her little niche, muddy as she hadn't been since infancy, safe with his heavy arm thrown over her, and that craggy face so close that her eyes could hardly focus.

The thunderstorm, a harsh black coil in the centre of the grey stormclouds, drifted by, heading north towards El Obeid. 'Almost clear,' he told her. 'I think we've——'

But the storm, perverse as all storms, had one final blow to strike. The largest bolt of lightning with which it was armed slashed back at them, smashed into the acacia trees, wasted the grove and all its contents, then the storm bubbled gently away, to be succeeded by a steady quiet downpour.

'Oh, my God,' gritted Ryan. 'Will you look at that?' Their tent had caught fire, two trees had fallen on top of the Land Rover, and flame was flickering around the vehicle's petrol tank.

'And all our food is in that truck!' he groaned. 'Why me, God?'

'It's not you, it's me,' Mattie said in anguish. 'Everything I've done on this trip has turned into——'

There was no need to complete the statement. The fire flicked a spark at the rear end of the truck, fell into a pool of petrol leaking around the tree-branch that had smashed a hole in the tank, and with a roar the truck, tentage, and what remained of the trees blossomed into a fireball and was gone.

Mattie struggled up to watch, only to have her head forced down violently into the mud. 'Damn fool!' Ryan raged. 'There's debris flying all over the place!' She sneaked a hand up in the general direction of her nose to clear it of mud. Breathing was necessary even when one was frightened half to death. And in another minute the storm had gone on to share its wrath with the rest of the world.

The steady drizzle kept up. Silence returned to their world. Ryan's hand pulled her up, and they both sat in the *wadi*, up to their waists in rushing water, and stared at their former encampment.

'Oh, my God,' he repeated mournfully.

'There's one good thing about it,' Mattie said calmly as she fished around underwater for her boots.

'Oh?' he growled. 'What's that, Mary Poppins?'

'Well, since we have to walk, isn't it convenient that the next village is only a mile or so away?'

'Not scared, are you?'

'Of course not.' She fumbled around in her clothing to find something to wipe the mud off her face. 'No sense being afraid after the fact, is there?'

'I suppose not,' he agreed gloomily.

'But five minutes ago,' she confessed, 'I was so scared my teeth were about to break from chattering! How does my hair look?'

'Muddy, like the rest of you. I thought rainwater made the perfect shampoo?'

'You men are all alike. You never will understand women!' Mattie smiled pertly at him. 'Why were you so gloomy a moment ago?'

'You women are all alike,' he returned. 'You never understand what's important to a man. I left my best pipe on the front seat of that car!'

CHAPTER SIX

'THERE'S nothing more comfortable than this,' Mattie sighed, leaning back into the straw, nibbling on a long blade of grass. The wooden wheels on the ancient oxcart squealed as they bounced slowly down the track between the mountains. 'And what a clever idea—to rent a whole team!' She hardly meant it as an outstanding compliment—after all, there hadn't been any other means of transportation in the village to rent or buy or steal!

She looked over at Ryan for a response, and stifled a giggle. Ryan Quinn, lying beside her in the straw on his stomach, was fast asleep. 'I don't know *why* I pick on you so much,' she muttered. 'You've certainly done your best to take care of me, in spite of my occasional stupidities!' He stirred, but only far enough to dislodge a fly perched on his nose.

Mattie grinned, and took off her hat to use it as a fan. The *serut* flies were not thick about them, but they were persistent. The oxen, animals with no future to speak of, refused to hurry. As a result their passage created no breezes, turned away no itinerant insects or mosquitoes. From time to time, the mismatched pair pulling the wagon would wander to a stop, as if they had forgotten just what they were about. Ndunonp, the boy who was hired as driver, walked far ahead of the team. He was too young to ogle the girls at the roadside, but he had a lively interest in every living thing on the road, except for the oxen.

Mattie looked around her, and took a deep breath. The air was clear and invigorating. In their second day of travel so far rain had pounded down for one. Not the whole day, by any means. Seldom did the downpour last for more than an hour or two, but when it *did* rain, it was done with enthusiasm. The country around her had sprung to life on the second day. The dried brown savannah grass had turned green, spruced itself up, and joined a collection of quickly blooming flowers. The seemingly dead bushes had sprouted. Little dry *wadis* had suddenly become creeks and streams. And, everywhere they went, little groups of Masakin were hard at work on their and their neighbours' fields.

On that first day Mattie had been terribly tense. She remembered vividly standing at the site of their camp while the gentle rains cleansed her of mud. Warm, gentle rain, like an outdoor shower. Unable to move, drowning in despair, she had watched while Ryan combed through the debris, looking for anything salvageable. As he came across small items he would hurl them out of the fire area at her feet. They made a comforting little pile. Two canteens, one half full of water. But then, water wasn't a problem any more, was it? One bedroll, slightly scorched, but usable. No extra clothing, except for her hat, which she had lost in the mad run for the *wadi*. She crammed it thankfully on her head. There was nothing more dangerous to a Caucasian head than Equatorial sunshine. One backpack, with a broken strap. One rifle, with part of its wooden stock burned away, but otherwise useful—or so Ryan said. One first-aid kit, a blessing beyond compare. One groundsheet, all that was left of the tent. One toothbrush to share between them.

Not much to possess, out here in the middle of the African plain. Ryan came out of the ashes and stood beside her, glaring at the tiny pile of effects. Mattie smiled at him. 'It certainly cuts down on the load we have to carry, doesn't it?'

He pushed back his own bush hat and scratched the top of his head, puzzled. 'I don't think I'll ever understand you,' he commented. 'I expected nothing less than a full-blown case of hysteria, and instead you're making jokes. What's *with* you, lady?'

'Why should I have hysterics? We may be lost, but we know what continent we're on. We're both healthy. There must be *some* food to be gleaned along the road, and besides, I have *you* with me.' And how in the world did that get in there? she asked herself. I have *you* with me? What kind of soft-hearted approach is that? A real leader has to keep some distance from her troops! But then, her conscience nagged, there are only two of us. We don't need followers and leaders, we just need— companions. Good companions! A smile ghosted around the corners of her mouth as she looked up at Ryan.

Not exactly handsome. The mud was still caked here and there on his broad face. His forehead was blackened from the smoke, but the rain was working on it. His dark hair was glued smoothly to his head by the moisture. His clothes were a mess. And yet he looked—capable.

'If that's a compliment, I thank you,' he said cautiously.

'It is,' laughed Mattie. 'Bend down here a little.'

Ryan searched her pixie face for a moment, then complied. She still had to stand on tiptoe, but she managed to rub a small segment of his cheek clean, and kissed it. He straightened up. She could see that wary look in his eyes.

'What was that for?' he asked.

'Oh—does there have to be a reason?'

'Well——' he pondered for a moment, then shrugged his shoulders, 'I suppose not. But thank you, anyway. I think we'd better be going. I'd like us to reach the village before dark sets in.'

A tiny excitement built up within her. She could not identify it, but there it was. 'You look like something the cat dragged in,' she teased.

Ryan straightened up, and a smile tugged at the corner of his mouth. 'While you, on the other hand, look nice enough to eat!'

It was Mattie's turn to be puzzled. Stone-heart Quinn, paying compliments? Her usually flexible mind refused to function. She watched as he dropped to his knees and began to assemble their worldly goods into a pack.

'I could help carry something,' she insisted as he swung the pack on his back.

'Sure you could,' he said curtly, then stopped as he saw the hurt in her eyes. 'Hey, I didn't mean anything by that. It's just that I was raised in a different—generation, I guess. Men carry the burdens. When I take a lady out to dinner, I pay. I hold doors open——'

'Around here?' Mattie interrupted, laughing. They both scanned their horizon, where neither house nor door intruded. He grinned back at her.

'So come on,' he chuckled. 'As soon as I *find* a door, I'll hold it open for you.' He hitched and flexed his muscles to set the pack in the most comfortable place, and started walking.

Mattie followed along as best she could. Her boots were waterproof, but only against moisture from their outside. Now they squeaked. Her skirt had not profited from the day's adventure, either. As the drizzle tapered off and the sun reappeared, steam rose from her clothes, and the skirt tightened around her knees as the cloth shrank. She struggled to adjust the waistband to give her more freedom, but fell farther behind. Finally, in desperation, she shouted, 'Hey!'

Ryan stopped and turned around. 'Trouble?'

'Not really. It's just—I need a minute to get things on right. I can't keep up at this speed.' It wasn't a complaint, just a statement of fact, and she presented it that way.

'OK,' he agreed. 'I keep forgetting. We're really not in any hurry, are we?'

'No,' she answered, twisting at her skirt, checking the laces of her boots. When her head came up, she had the feeling that she had just learned something tremendously important. We're really not in any hurry! Not since her childhood, when she and Mary-Kate would go walking, had she not been in any hurry. Her ambitions and loves had driven her through school at high speed. Always trying to be the best—in everything she did. And succeeding. How many times had her mother said, 'Slow down, girl! There's a long life ahead of you. You don't have to live all your years in the first twenty!'?

When they started off together, side by side, Ryan set a slower pace. They walked around the curve of the foothills, the massive peak of Jebel Koalib staring down at them. Mattie stumbled on loose stones, and his hand seized hers to steady her. But when they started off again, he was still clutching her hand. And for some reason she was reluctant to break the contact herself.

It took them an hour to climb the little ridge in front of them, and there, on the floor of the valley, was the village, a little cluster of huts. But it wasn't the village that surprised her. It was the sun, setting in vari-coloured glory on the hills to their west. She pulled Ryan to a stop, awed by the nature painting.

'Look at that!' she gasped.

He looked up just as the gold turned to amber, the red to purple. 'Good lord!' he exclaimed. They stood and watched as the colours changed, merged, then were gone into the twilight. 'Isn't that strange?' said Ryan.

'I've been on this job for months, and that's the first time I've had the time to look at a sunset. Beautiful, huh?'

Mattie squeezed his hand for an answer, too filled by the glory of the African world to speak. Not for another ten minutes did they start off down the hill again, to a welcome they had never anticipated.

It was a *little* village, no doubt about that. But if its population was four hundred, then they must have sent out to recruit relatives. At least that was what it looked like, Mattie thought. There must be a thousand people here, all cheerily waiting, smiling. These were the Masakin Tiwal, the tall Nubians. The crowd began to chant, and a few of the men began the great hopping dance that sent them towering above their neighbours like huge storks searching the shallows.

'You *do* speak Tiwal?' she asked nervously.

'A few words,' Ryan muttered. 'Hello, how are you— that kind of stuff.'

'That will be a big help, I'm sure,' she returned. 'Try a little something on this big guy in the front of the crowd.'

They hadn't done too badly at all, she told herself an hour later. The big fellow's name was Amepa. He had three wives, a great many cattle, and an order from Chief Artafi to wait and welcome the Latimore representatives.

'How long?' Mattie whispered. 'They surely didn't expect us to walk? How did they know we were coming? How long would they have waited?'

'It hardly matters,' Ryan told her. 'The bush tele-graph told the Chief we were coming. As far as *these* people are concerned, *how long* never enters into it. They wait until we come, or until the Chief tells them to stop waiting. It simplifies life a great deal, doesn't it? Dig these crazy houses!'

The huts in the village were all identical. Five adobe round towers with thatched conical roofs were joined together in a star shape by an adobe wall, to make a single home. Each tower had its own purpose: this one a sleeping room, that one for storage, another for the children, and so forth. The central courtyard provided space for an open cooking fire. 'Amepa has a tough time,' Ryan observed. 'He has to provide an identical house for each of his three wives. That's why most tribesmen have only one—wife, that is. Want to take a shower?'

'I surely do,' Mattie responded, 'but only if you're out of the house, Mr Quinn.' Which brought another grin to his face as he walked out.

The shower was a surprise that was easily solved. One section of the courtyard was paved with stone. Directly above, set in the wall on a gimbal, was a large pot of water. The drill, explained in pantomime by a young girl who stayed to help, required that Mattie strip, step under the pot, tilt it over until water spilled over her, stop to soap up with a harsh lye soap, then rinse the same way. It felt good. She used the soap lavishly, and dried herself on a heavy cotton towel when done.

Her clothes were a mess, and she hated to put them back on. The decision was taken from her; after the shower she found they had all disappeared, to be replaced by a white *gallabiya* that covered her from neck to ankle. One size fits all, she told herself as she shrugged her way into the soft cotton. Her assistant, who was dressed tastefully in tribal markings and nothing else, tugged the hem of the *gallabiya* into place and led her by the hand to the house next door. Ryan was waiting for her, dressed incongruously in a pair of European-style red shorts.

'Dinner,' he said, eyeing her up one side and down the other. 'Don't you look all the style!'

'You, too,' she told him. 'Turn around and let me see the back.'

He did a quick pirouette. 'Satisfied?'

'Hmm.' He was a great deal of man. She hadn't noticed that before. Solidly built—almost square, with not an ounce of fat on him. The kind of man you see in swimwear advertisements. Yummy, her sister Faith would say. Mattie could hardly muster enough words about it to make an intelligent statement. It was the sort of thing she had never given much thought to, there had just never been enough time. And yet, just looking, she felt bereft— as if she had missed something while she was growing up.

'Dinner?' Ryan queried. 'Our host can't eat with us. We're the Chief's guests, and he's only a local headman.'

They ate from a common dish, a wooden platter piled high with gleaming white rice, intermixed with vegetables. Lentils, beans, onions—Mattie could identify these, but the rest escaped her.

'No meat?' she asked.

'It's not something on the normal menu,' he returned. 'Fish, if they live near the river. Or occasionally, for a big feast. Like it?'

'It tastes fine, but I'm having trouble getting it to my mouth. What happened to the knife and fork and spoon bit?'

'Only for sissies,' he said solemnly. 'You eat with the right hand—three fingers, actually. Stick them into the food, twirl it around to make a little ball, and stuff it into your mouth.'

'No wonder they eat naked,' Mattie sighed after her third try. 'I'm making a mess of somebody's gown.'

'Persistence, lady.'

'Yeah, persistence.' But she was able to laugh at herself, and finally got the hang of it. By now, total darkness had descended. The fire burning on the hearth and a torch stuck into the wall at the gate were the only lights. Above them the stars watched—and probably laughed their fill. She washed her hands under the shower head, dried them on her *gallabiya*, and stretched.

'Tired?' queried Ryan.

'Stiff,' she admitted.

'Wouldn't care for a walk in the moonlight?'

She looked down at her battered boots. All signs of smartness had gone. At home in Darkest Africa, she laughed to herself. Mattie Latimore, in field boots and a nightgown! If Ma could only see me now!

'Don't believe I do,' she answered. 'I think I'd better save my feet for tomorrow. Sleep is what I need most. Where?'

'Well, this is our house,' he began slowly. 'There's only one sleeping room, and we've only got one sleeping-bag with us.'

By the light of the flickering fire, there was something devilish about him—perhaps the little peaks of his eyebrows. One on either side, they gave just an indication of horns. 'No other way, I suppose?' she queried.

'No other way,' he confirmed. 'Besides, these good people think——' He paused, fishing for the right word.

'Go ahead,' she urged. 'This is no time to be a coward.'

'Well,' he stammered, 'they were told that a chief and his woman would be coming, and——'

'OK, OK. And I suppose that of us two, you're the chief?'

'Damn right,' he muttered. 'And you're my woman! And don't argue!'

'Who's arguing?' Mattie said mildly as she made her way into the sleeping hut.

There was a platform along one side of the hut. Adobe, as the rest of the house, with no adornments, and a battered sleeping-bag stretched out on its top. The same sleeping-bag she had first met on the *Hurriya*. Mattie took a couple of deep breaths to settle her nerves. Things were not as bad here as on that first night on the boat. She had fallen into a fantasy world, where nothing seemed to be like home, and its very strangeness suppressed her fears. Without giving it a thought, she unlaced her boots, set them aside, and slid into the bag.

An hour later, Ryan came in and joined her. 'Enough room?' she asked drowsily as he settled down. He grunted a non-reply and turned on his side, his back to her. Within minutes, Mattie could hear his breathing slow. Asleep, she told herself, almost there herself. Asleep. I'm glad. I'd hate to try to out-wrestle him all night. But she really wasn't all that glad. Not that she wanted an all-out combat, but he could have made a small pass at her, couldn't he? How's that for puncturing a girl's ego! Before she could analyse her feelings, she too fell asleep.

Mattie awoke at dawn, fumbling for an awareness. She was warm, comfortable, lying on her left side. Ryan was pressed up against her back, one of his arms thrown across her stomach. There was no way she could move the arm without awakening him, and she didn't want to do that. He had had a hard time the day before. He would undoubtedly have a hard day today. And he needed his rest. The argument didn't sound half bad to her, and it allowed her to ignore the signals her body was sending. Stop kidding, her conscience dictated. You like it!

'Shut up,' she muttered. The words were like the beat of a conductor's baton. Ryan came instantly awake, ready for anything. Half a dozen voices in the courtyard began a giggling conversation, and two heads stuck through the doorway of the hut and said something.

'Breakfast,' Ryan translated. 'You OK?'

Mattie reached out a hand in his direction to support herself, then yelped as her fingers struck bare skin. 'Yes, I'm all right,' she gasped. The hand bounced away from the fire of him, and hung in mid-air with no place to go. He grinned as he slid out of the sleeping-bag. He was still wearing those ridiculous red shorts.

Mattie followed him warily. The *gallabiya* had crept up while she slept, riding high on her hips. In the bright morning sun, she had no intention of displaying *that* much leg. It took some doing. Although she kept her eye on Ryan constantly, he seemed to ignore her. Her own regular clothing was stacked by the bed, all washed and neatly folded. Her boots had been cleaned and oiled with some sweet-smelling fragrance, and she slipped them on.

Breakfast was in the form of flat bread, fried on the iron that served as skillet, then folded around a handful of the same vegetables she had seen the night before. Hot tea topped it off.

'And now what do we do?' she asked as she stuffed herself with the last morsel of bread.

'The same as always,' Ryan returned. 'We go to Topari.'

'But that must be miles away!'

'About eighty,' he agreed amiably.

'I can't——' she started to say, then clamped her lips together. All I need to do is say I can't walk that far, she told herself bitterly, and he'll start with that *little woman* line. So I can't walk eighty miles—I'm darned if I'll tell him that. Ryan surprised her.

'We ride—all the way,' he told her.

'Ride? Ride what?'

'Your carriage awaits,' he laughed, and gestured towards the door. And there they were: one two-wheeled wooden cart, two tired oxen, a container of rancid animal fat to grease the axles with, and one bright-faced little boy, all surrounded by the entire village population, waiting to see them off.

'We're going to Topari in *that*?' gasped Mattie.

'Yup. They filled it with fresh straw, just for us.'

'But that'll take for ever to go eighty miles!'

'I'm assured that these are two fine extra-powerful oxen,' Ryan said solemnly. 'Ten miles a day—an eight-day trip! The ladies have a gift for you. Smile.'

Mattie smiled. The villagers began to sing as he helped her up into the cart. The oxen made vague moves forward, paying no attention at all to the little round-faced boy and his big stick. An hour later they could still hear the singing back in the village. Mattie lay back in the straw and laughed. At herself, her world, at Ryan, and all their pretensions.

On that first day, they hardly made their ten miles. The oxen preferred other paths. One of the wheels came loose and had to be repaired. Ryan handled it all with an equanimity that surprised her. Every time she objected, he would say, 'There's no hurry.' And by the end of the day, huddled around a dung fire, eating the same sort of bread they had had for breakfast, Mattie was beginning to believe it.

'I didn't realise you could cook,' he said. 'This bread is great.'

'Of course,' she admitted grandly. 'It's one of the requirements of being a Latimore girl.'

'Cooking?'

'You'd better believe it, mister. Although I must say, I haven't made bread this way before.'

'So how did you learn?'

'I watched the women at breakfast, then told myself it was just like making pancakes.' And then she added wistfully, 'I sure would like a steak sandwich.'

'Not good for you,' he pontificated. 'Vegetarian diets are healthy!'

'I'm sure they are,' she sighed. 'And boring. We didn't get very far today.'

'No caravan ever does,' he said. 'The first twenty-four hours is always the shakedown time. We'll do better tomorrow. Where's the boy?'

'I fed him earlier. He's over there with the oxen. Are you *sure* those are high-speed bullocks?'

'That's what I was told,' he assured her. 'You don't suppose we were dealing with the only con man in the Masakin tribe?'

Mattie laughed—threw back her head, let her lovely blonde hair blow in the wind, and laughed. And when she stopped Ryan was staring at her, a strange, hungry expression on his face.

Quick, her mind told her, change the subject! 'I wish I could have another shower,' she said quietly.

'No showers, but we have a bathtub,' he reminded her.

'You mean that watering-hole? I thought it might be contaminated with something.'

'No reason why it should be, Mattie.' Her name came out gently, with none of the sarcasm he had used earlier. 'That was a dry *wadi* not more than three days ago. It's filled with rainwater. What more could you ask? Good for the complexion, pure rainwater is, isn't it?'

'It surely is,' she said bravely. 'Soap?'

'We brought plenty.'

'I wish I had another *gallabiya*. I'd like to save my good clothes until we make our entrance.'

'The ladies just happened to stuff three or four in that bag for you. And a couple of towels. And a comb. What more could you ask?'

Push your luck, Mattie told herself. 'I'm a little—well, it's a big open area, and there could be wild animals, and——'

'And what else do you need?' Ryan was standing too close to be avoided. Mattie was a woman who required her own personal space around her, but for once she didn't mind being crowded.

'I think I need a guard,' she half whispered.

'I'm available,' he offered.

'I didn't mean someone to stand there and watch me bathe,' she snapped hurriedly. 'I don't want you to——'

'Get the wrong idea?' he interrupted. 'Me take advantage of the boss-lady?'

'Well,' she offered apologetically, 'I just wanted everything to be—clear.'

'You bet. Anything else?'

They walked over to the *wadi* together, past the oxen, leaving the tiny circle of fire. Mattie sat on the bank and watched as Ryan made a careful inspection. 'Nothing,' he reported. 'All clear. Go ahead.'

'Yeah,' she replied. 'Just as soon as you——'

'I'm going,' he assured her. 'I'm going.'

He faded away into the darkness. She watched, not too confident about him—or herself. Just to be sure, the moment he disappeared she began to count backwards from a hundred, and not until she had come down to zero did she stand up, carefully strip down, fumble for the soap, and test the water.

Expecting New England cold, she got African warm. The water swelled up around her soothingly as she waded out. It was deep enough to come almost to her breasts. She stood for an uneasy moment, scanning the horizon, but nothing moved. 'Too many Frank Buck movies on television,' she muttered. 'There aren't any lions at *this* watering-hole. And why in the world would Ryan want to stare at *me*? For the last two days he's seen nothing but naked women. Some pretty cute ones, too.' The soap was applied vigorously, as if she were trying to rub out the thought of Ryan Quinn and naked women. Twice she lost the bar, and it was *not* loaded with air bubbles to make it float.

Diving became a little game until she rescued the precious soap and waded out to drop it by her pile of clothing. Then back into the water for a brisk swim. Riding an oxcart, while pleasant, was also a problem. Four or five times during the day she had got down to walk, outdistancing the oxen with little trouble at all. And now the joy of swimming in the buff made her little world—well, not perfect, but certainly contented.

Strange, Mattie told herself as she waded out to the shore. I feel better now than I can remember in years! Everything is so—casual. Life has ceased to be a race. I'm riding to Topari, and the going is important, not the getting there. She glared up at the moon, which had just surprised her. Silver light spun across warm water, almost bright enough to set shadows. She shook her head and laughed as water sprayed around her from the golden hair. One misstep put her down on her knees in the water. She laughed again, a soft series of notes that climbed the scale from her contralto voice, then dropped down again. 'See,' she whispered to the world, 'you've always been too proud of your hair, and pride goeth before a fall!'

Water was streaming down from that hair into her eyes as she fumbled blindly out on to the hardpan that surrounded the *wadi*, and stretched in the moonlight. 'Aphrodite,' a male voice said in her ear, and she whirled around, to find herself wound up in one of the soft cotton towels, gifts from the village of Moro.

'Ryan?' she yelped in alarm.

'Who else?'

She tried to pull away from him, but his hands were on her shoulders, holding her against him. One of his hands was drawing great circles across her back, from her shoulders to her pert, round hips.

'What are you doing?' she whispered.

'Drying your back. What else?'

She had never felt anything like this in all her life. Oh, Ma had dried her back many a time when she was young, but nothing had felt like this. There was an excitement building up in her that *had* to be ended, and quickly. She twisted away from him, losing the towel in the doing, leaving her standing in the moonlight, hands crossed over her breasts in that age-old gesture.

'You promised you'd *guard* me,' she quavered.

'I am,' he pointed out. 'You've lost your towel.'

'You—you said you'd keep your distance!' she wailed.

'I lied,' he returned sombrely.

She could have run. She could have screamed. She could have raged. Instead she stood still, shivering as the cool night wind caressed her wet body. Ryan moved close again and, as gently as anyone could, wrapped her in the towel.

'Better?' he asked, his hands busy drying her hair. There were too many sensations upsetting her analytical mind. Too many throbbing signals from her senses, telling her—what? And that was the trouble. She could not interpret the messages!

Ryan turned her around and began to dry her front, gently moving his hands over the towel and over her breasts, and now she could read the messages. 'Danger!' That was the signal coming in from all directions. Mattie backed away from him, and inadvertently opened a gap in the towel.

'Beautiful,' he said softly as he gazed down at her perky little breasts, standing prouder than they had ever stood before. And then, regretfully, 'Beautiful,' as he closed the gap, kissed her gently on the forehead, and stepped back.

For another moment they faced each other, outlined by moonlight but not revealed. Then Ryan shook himself.

'Put your boots on before you come back,' he warned. 'There may be all kinds of things to stumble over.' She could see his impassive face as he stared, then he turned away and started to walk towards the pinpoint of light that was their fire.

'Boots,' she muttered as she shook herself, and sat down on her pile of clothes to slip her feet into the leather protection. 'Boots.' She shivered, but was not cold. Another of the white *gallabiyas* slid over her head. She tugged it down over her hips, gathered up her paraphernalia, and stopped for one more look at the moonlit path across the gleaming water. A star laughed down at her. 'Lord knows how many seductions *you've* seen,' she sighed up at it. 'Remember to keep a distance between yourself as the boss, and your employees! Right out of the company handbook. Damn you, Mr Quinn!'

CHAPTER SEVEN

THE THIRD DAY of their long trek started at sunrise in a distinctly cool mood. Rain had come again, held off their backs by stretching the rescued groundsheet over a rope tied across the cart's axis as a sort of tent. The little boy who had been their guide disappeared.

'That's his home village over there,' Ryan pointed out. 'We pick up a new guide in an hour or so.'

'Thank you, Mr Quinn,' Mattie said bleakly.

'Mr Quinn? After last night?'

'Mr Quinn *because* of last night.' She had her own favourite little hollow in the straw, all scooped out to fit. To emphasise her disapproval she gave it up—reluctantly—and moved to the back of the cart. The rain lasted about two hours. Their coolness only made it through half an hour.

'Look, I'm sorry if I—caused you any problem,' Ryan apologised. It was just the break for which Mattie was looking.

'It was no trouble,' she told him. 'Not really. You surprised me, and like all creatures I tend to strike out at surprises. And I was embarrassed, too, if you must know.' She struggled to push a smile to her lips. It trembled a bit, but made it.

'I didn't realise you had dimples,' he commented. 'Coming back up front?'

'I believe I will.' Mattie scrambled up the slope of the cart to her favoured spot. 'It's not much fun playing kee-bird.'

'Kee-bird?'

116

'Old New England joke,' she chuckled. 'The kee-bird flies backwards so it can see where it's been, and as it flies it yells *kee*—oops!'

It earned her another grin. Good lord, she thought, he's almost handsome when he smiles! She lay back with that thought in mind, and promptly fell asleep.

She woke at noon. Ryan was sitting cross-legged beside her, staring at the oxen. The rain was still coming down, and the animals had decided they'd had enough. Regardless of commands, they wandered off the road into the savannah grass and were grazing. 'Midday. Time for lunch?' Mattie speculated. Ryan looked at his wristwatch.

'Six o'clock,' he announced with a grin. She took a startled look at her own watch, a gift from her father which wouldn't dare be wrong.

'You didn't set it for local time,' he told her, leaning over to see. There was a flicker of shock as his arm grazed her breast. She could smell the warm maleness of him. Somewhere she had read an article which said that odour was one of the prime components of human sexuality. At the moment, she could not deny it.

'I—set it by your camp clock back at Kosti,' she told him.

'That's fine, but now we're in Nuba land, and time here is measured by the sun. Dawn is the first daytime hour, and eleven follow. Sunset is the first night hour.'

'But then the hours can't be all the same length?'

'Sure they can,' he said. 'We're only a few degrees from the Equator, you know. There may be a small difference in the length of hours, but the Masakin hardly care, so we shouldn't. Now, since you're the boss, and in the Latimore kingdom the boss does the dirty work——'

'Just a darn minute,' Mattie snapped. 'The Latimore kingdom is a long way behind us. We're equal partners!'

'Well, in that case, *partner*, we'll flip a coin to see which one of us goes out in the rain to get the oxen back on the road again.'

She took a quick look out from under their shelter. 'You wouldn't ask a *woman* to go out in that storm, would you?' she pleaded.

'Ah! We're *not* equal,' chuckled Ryan. 'Somehow or another, I knew that would come up. You're not one of the new feminists?'

'Well,' she stalled, 'I am, and then I'm not. I hold to my mother's thesis. She's against the equality movement. She says she'll be darned if she's ever going to admit that any man is as good as she is!'

'Oh, boy,' he moaned. 'An ultra-feminist!'

'Not really,' Mattie sighed. 'I believe men and women are complementary. Like my mother and father.'

'In that case, I tell you what I'll do.' One of Ryan's big fingers came over and tilted her head up. 'I'll make the sacrifice. *I'll* go out in the rain and the mud and get soaked and start our cart again, providing you pay me for my trouble.' Mattie stared at him, her blue eyes as round as plates. He was up to something, and she didn't know what.

'All right,' she agreed hesitantly.

He vaulted over the top bar of the cart. She stretched out on her stomach to watch the exercise. The oxen were not quite ready. It was hard not to laugh, watching him, rain-soaked, as he prodded and pushed, and eventually moved around to the animals' heads and gave them a lecture, including arm-waving and fist-threatening.

'Don't hit the poor beasts!' she shouted at him. He glared back at her, made one final effort, and the two animals, deciding for themselves that it was time to go, ambled back to the road and began their perambulation. Moments later Ryan tumbled into the cart, water streaming down his face.

'Look at me,' he grumbled as he fished through the pack for a towel to wipe his hair. 'I need gills to survive out there!' He threw the towel over a handy peg and sprawled out beside her. 'And now then, my pretty——'

'What the devil are you—hey, you're all wet!' she exclaimed as he pulled her out of her little nest and into his arms. 'What do you think you're doing?'

'Collecting my pay.'

'I—don't have my purse,' she gabbled. 'You'll—I can't pay you right now. I don't have——'

'You have everything you need.'

She ducked her head away as he loomed over her, but there was nowhere to go. She lay partially under him, her breasts crushed against his soaking shirt, one of his legs over hers, pinning her to the straw. He was so close that he went out of focus. She shut her eyes. Why struggle? her conscience harried her. You know you want it! It's only a kiss, I think! And anyway, the best defence is a good offence.

It was that last sentence that dictated her actions. When said quickly, it sounded almost logical. Both her arms wriggled out of Ryan's bear-hug, and her hands met and locked at the nape of his neck, even before his lips feather-touched hers. He was drawing back when he felt the pressure as she tried to hold her head in position. That first touch had been a lovely taste. When he came back it was like an attack by Attila the Hun, set to ravage a soft mouth which had no objections. The feelings continued for what seemed like hours, driving little spurts of fever up her spine, but eventually Ryan stopped and pulled away. From the far corner of the wagon he searched her face sombrely.

It took time for Mattie to get her breathing apparatus under control. Time to re-establish the analytical Miss Latimore—the engineer. Ryan seemed to be reading her face as she turned from one personality to the other.

'I suppose this makes me *persona non grata*?' he asked cautiously.

Mattie gave him one of her best smiles. 'Not on my account,' she said pertly. 'I enjoyed it. Didn't you?'

In his best Texas drawl he said, 'Well, ma'am, ah do believe ah did. Care for another?'

She chose her words very carefully, recognising a turning-point when she came to it. 'I don't believe so, Mr Quinn. It's the sort of thing a girl can enjoy in small quantities, but I wouldn't want to make a habit of it. But I did enjoy the one.'

'I see. Don't call us, we'll call you?'

'That's approximately right,' she said primly. 'But that doesn't mean we can't be friends. Good friends.'

Ryan shrugged his shoulders, grinning. 'Best offer I've had this week, lady.'

Probably the only one, Mattie told herself. I really ought to be mad at him. I really ought. So why aren't I? There was no answer, even though she poked in all the crowded corners of her brain. She offered him another smile, rolled over on her stomach, and watched the tails of the two oxen twitching back and forth, back and forth, until she grew drowsy.

The days that followed were like a spring pattern in a rose garden. The little bud nourished that day expanded, opened, and spread an aura of contentment over their pilgrimage. The oxen continued at their stated pace. They picked up a new guide for the trip, an older warrior, whose name they never did learn, and they fell into the companionable rhythm that such travel required.

Ryan made the fires each night and morning, saw to the oxen, turned the straw over in the cart to keep down mildew, and treated Mattie with all the kind accord one might expect from a friendly uncle. Except for those inadvertent times when he touched her. Mere accidents, of course, due to the narrow confines of the cart. But every touch awakened a memory, reinvigorated a spark that caused Mattie's face to take on a glow of excitement that lasted all day.

The next day, under a clear sky, they walked together, outdistancing the oxen without even trying. 'It's safer to walk in front of them than behind,' Ryan teased.

They held hands like teenagers, she laughing up into his dark eyes, he wearing that small smile that was his emblem of happiness. Beside the road, they came on a cluster of little yellow flowers.

'Daisies,' he said quickly, and picked two of the blossoms.

Mattie knew they were not, but it hardly mattered. They were a full hundred paces ahead of the cart, and the oxen had stopped. He held his blossom up in front of her, and began plucking at the petals. 'She loves me, she loves me not,' until the poor little flower was barren on 'she loves me'.

'Now, how did you do that?' she asked, laughing.

'I counted them before I started, and discarded the petal that didn't fit.'

'But that's cheating!' she gasped.

'Not a bit,' he maintained. 'All's fair in love and war!'

It isn't funny, she told herself. Ryan was standing in front of her, watching with those keen hawk eyes. Love and war? This certainly wasn't war, so it must be——? He was waiting for her to say something!

Unsure of her own newborn emotions, she said, 'Our oxen are on strike,' and winced as she saw the expectant smile fade from his face.

They became storytellers. She told him all the little details of her life as one of the daughters of the Latimore house. He told her all about life on a windswept cattle ranch in the Texas panhandle, and how he, after the loss of his father, did his best to keep the ranch going while he studied at the University of Texas for his engineering degree.

'I always wanted to wander,' he said moodily one night. 'But now—I don't know. I have the feeling that it's time to put my roots down.'

'Go back to Texas, you mean?' They were lying side by side in the straw, faces turned to the open sky, close to twilight.

'Probably,' he said. 'I don't suppose *you* could take to that kind of life?'

'Oh, I don't know. The best years of my life were on a farm, when my father married my stepmother.'

'That's the first time I ever heard you say that,' Ryan commented. 'Stepmother, I mean. I thought she was your natural mother. Wicked stepmother?'

'Don't you believe it,' laughed Mattie. 'More like a fairy godmother. My pop had no idea what to do with a seven-year-old girl child. My sister Becky is Mary-Kate's daughter. Man, did we both push them to the altar!'

'And now you're an engineer?'

'Well—from force of circumstances,' she told him. 'I'm really qualified as an architect—but Pop needed a hand in the business. My brother Michael will take it all over some day, but he's only—lord, Mike is twelve years old. It was only yesterday he was a baby!'

'A girl could do a lot of architecting on the porch of my ranch. Plenty of space, lots of comfort——'

'And Virginia,' she interrupted.

'Yeah, Virginia,' he muttered. After a moment of silence she patted his wrist comfortingly and climbed down out of the cart to see about supper.

He came back to her after putting the oxen out to graze. She had managed the fire for herself. A few handfuls of dried straw, one or two dried dung patties gathered up by their Masakin guide during the day, all made a tiny but hot fire to cook their simple meal.

'Getting pretty handy,' Ryan complimented. 'I should have noticed there was a farm girl inside that beautiful skin.'

'Get away with you!' Mattie laughed. 'I know the blarney when I hear it, even from a Texas cowboy. Another two days and my skin is going to be so tanned it'll crack. This soap is bleaching my hair from strawberry to silver. Lord, what a mess I am!'

'Just the kind of mess a man likes to mess with,' he chuckled, squeezing her arm. The phrase—and the thought—stuck with Mattie through her dreams that night. Long, involved dreams, that would have had to be rated 'X' by the Hollywood Review Board.

It was their last night on the road. All during the day they had been passed by large and small bands of Masakin, all heading in the same direction. Warriors, herdboys, women, little children, they strolled down the road singing and chanting, a happy gathering, moving towards the festival centre at Topari.

'I think we'd better stop here for the night.' Ryan surveyed the stream of people going by. 'There's water and plenty of space. I suspect if we get any closer to the village we won't find either.'

'About how far do you think we would have to go tomorrow?' Mattie asked.

'Not far. Three—maybe four miles, according to our guide.'

'I'm all for it. Our last night on the road, so to speak. Don't you feel a little bit nervous?'

'A little bit,' he acknowledged. They both jumped down from the wagon and began their regular nightly procedures. Things went in their usual order, save only that sounds could be heard on the night winds— chanting, singing, a constant drum of dancing feet in such number as to thunder through the earth. Other pilgrims on the path disappeared, hurrying forwards to join the excitement.

After their meal they walked to the top of a tiny hillock nearby and waited to watch the moon rise, his arm around her shoulders, her arm around his waist.

'We've come a long way,' Mattie said softly.

Ryan squeezed her shoulder gently. 'Eighty miles, more or less.'

'I don't mean in miles. I mean—oh, you know.'

'Yes, I know. You've changed.'

'And so have you, thank God.'

'Now who's making smart remarks?' It was too dark to see, but she could *feel* him grinning down at her.

'I'm a little—scared about what comes next,' she sighed.

'With us? Let nature take its course.'

'No,' she remonstrated. 'With them, down in the village. Do you have any idea how to go about this?'

'A couple of vague ones,' he returned. 'We'll have to see how the cookie crumbles. And you?'

'I'm not sure. Somehow we have to involve the Masakin future with the future of the railroad. Somehow.'

'Leave it,' he advised. 'Sufficient unto the day, and all that.'

'How about that?' teased Mattie. 'A Bible-quoting Texan!'

'Thumping,' Ryan corrected cheerfully. 'A Bible-thumping Texan. Want to make something out of it?'

'Not me,' she confessed. 'But what I'd *like* to do is have another swim. Do you think it's possible?'

'Sure is,' he laughed. 'This thing isn't a water-hole, it's a *ghor*.'

'What the devil is a *ghor*?'

'It's a riverbed that's dry for half the year,' he explained. 'A sort of part-time creek. So when it's dry, the Sudanese build a dam across the lower end. The soil around here is heavy clay; it retains water. When the rains come, the *ghor* fills up behind the dam, and hey presto!—they have a reservoir. Let's both go and take a dip.'

'I—didn't bring a swimsuit,' she stammered.

'You've never been skinny-dipping?'

'Only—a long time ago,' she sighed. 'You really have no idea how deep my Calvinist roots go.'

'So we'll prune them a little. You go ahead, right down at the foot of this knoll. I'll go back, check on the oxen, and find a couple of towels.'

Mattie hesitated a moment after he had disappeared into the darkness. Only the stars were out; the moon would make an appearance in another half-hour, and in the meantime she seemed all alone on a distant planet. Moody, she told herself. You're a big girl now. Make up your mind!

It took Ryan ten minutes to make the trip. There was a white spot on the shore, marking the place where Mattie had left her clothes. Out in the middle distance there was a splash or two. He stripped quickly, and was about to take his own plunge when the moon came up, and painted a path directly across the man-made lake, highlighting her hair, and the flash of an alabaster arm as she did a slow backstroke. A silver lady on a silver sea, he thought, and for a moment was locked in position. What is she doing to me? He took a deep breath and dived in a shallow racing entrance, to ask her.

They slept late for a change, awaking only when the tramp of feet began, and the procession of pilgrims passed them by. Mattie opened one eye carefully. She was lying cuddled in the shelter of Ryan's arm, his free hand resting on her hip. Nothing happened last night, she assured herself fiercely. We swam, we played, he kissed me. He carried me back to the wagon. We dried each other—and that's all! He could have had more, but he didn't. And what does that mean, little girl?

She tried to get up without disturbing him, but failed. At the first slight movement of her head, both his eyes came open. It was like waking up next to a tiger, she thought.

'Well, what have we here?' he asked gently. 'A girl?'

'Time to get up,' she said flatly. 'The trip is over.'

'Ah, I get it. Cinderella was out too late and the carriage has turned back into a pumpkin?'

'Into an oxcart,' she corrected, wriggling out of his clasp. He watched as she dressed, lying there with hands clasped behind his head, but saying nothing. They went about their usual routine, but in a stiff and constrained manner. The ease and pleasure of the trip had gone, and the obligations of the Latimore Corporation had taken over. Twice Ryan stopped what he was doing and started to say something, only to swallow the words. Mattie looked up expectantly at each occasion, then hid her head to hide her mourning spirit. Mourning. Something had died in the early morning light, and she had no idea whether to or how to resurrect it.

They came to the top of the last rolling hill mid-morning—the fourth hour, in local time. Not a word had been said during all that time. Mattie sat with her legs dangling over the front of the cart. Ryan walked at the head of the oxen, urging them on. She watched his lithe figure so closely that she hardly noticed the crowds of pilgrims around them, all hurrying as *they* were not. The man seemed so—unapproachable, and yet she could not free her mind of those little intimacies they had shared on their eight-day trek across the countryside. For a time they had abdicated from the mad race of civilisation. They had cut a piece out of the hurly-burly, and made their own world, including only earth and sky and themselves. And now it was gone.

She looked down at herself, expecting to see the difference their sojourn had made, but Mattie Latimore seemed to be unchanged. She had put on her European clothing: the wrap-around beige skirt, the loose camisole, the almost-white blouse. Her lovely blonde hair was crammed up under her bush hat. Take away the oxen and I might as well be on Boston Common, she thought. But depression was not Mattie's thing. 'How stupid can you get?' she muttered to herself. 'Boston Common? Yuck! Look around you, lady.' And she did. Her mouth fell open, and Ryan chose just that moment to come back to the cart.

'Something wrong?' he asked gravely.

'I was—daydreaming,' she stammered. 'Look at the crowds!'

'It even surprises me,' he returned, climbing up to sit beside her. 'A few hundred men, I thought, to celebrate the festival and the council meeting. It must be a lot more important than *that*. I swear there must be eight—nine thousand people here!'

'And more coming,' she reported excitedly. The village of Topari, which consisted of about four hundred of those five-towered huts she had become accustomed to, was almost lost in the mass of tents and campsites and lean-tos that surrounded it. And yet, for all those thousands, there was hardly a noise. Occasionally a chicken or two squawked. A child cried and was hushed. The biggest noise to be heard was the squeaking of the wooden wheels of their oxcart.

In the barren centre of the village, a space about the size of a football field, thousands of orderly pilgrims had formed in an oblong, with an open space in the middle. There was not a tree in sight, but two huge umbrellas covered the head of the man seated in the middle of that open space.

'I've never seen anything like that in my life,' Mattie said nervously, and moved closer to Ryan's side. Almost unconsciously, he dropped an arm around her shoulders. 'I'm—a little shook up.'

'Not to worry,' he offered cheerfully. 'After all we've been through, what could they do to us?'

Keep it light, Mattie told herself. She rubbed her eyes with one knuckle and managed a little gurgle of laughter. 'You don't suppose they're cannibals?'

'Not this crowd,' he assured her. 'They were once the most feared warriors in Africa, but now they're a bunch of pussycats.'

'I'll bet they are. And every one of those pussycats is carrying a big long spear!'

'That could be a problem.' He gave her one of those lop-sided grins. 'You're a very tasty dish, Mattie.' It was the first time he had used her name that day, and it felt—nice. And it deserved a compliment in return.

'And you're a very nice man, Ryan,' she said. She looked away, to hide her eyes from his knowing inspection.

'Well,' he drawled. 'My first *real* compliment!' She stubbornly refused to look in his direction. 'And there's another first—a woman with all her clothes on!'

Her head snapped around. Curiosity had always been her downfall. And it was true. in the middle of the shifting, moving crowd, a young native girl was standing at the side of the road, dressed in skirt and blouse. She wore no shoes, but a gold chain circled her neck, and from it hung a cross!

'A Christian?' gasped Mattie.

'Not only that, but she's waiting for us,' Ryan returned. He vaulted over the side of the cart like a trained athlete. Mattie, stiff from too much riding, clumsily followed. The oxen, being the intelligent beasts they were, kept ambling along.

'Latimore,' the girl called to them. She pronounced it *Lateemore*, but the big smile on her face was welcome enough.

'Yes, Latimore,' said Ryan, repeating her own pronunciation.

'I am called Meriam,' she said, stepping forward to extend a hand. Her English was impeccable—an upper-class English accent lent charm. 'Because I speak English, the Chief has directed me to be your—translator. Is that the right word?'

'That's the right word,' Ryan affirmed. 'And this is——'

'Your woman?' Meriam interrupted. 'Come along. Leave those beasts. Everything is prepared.'

'Er—yes, Mattie is my woman.' And we could do with a little less pomposity, Mattie thought as she listened. My woman, indeed!

'You don't have to be so damn convincing,' she muttered in his ear.

'But you are young!' Meriam stared at Mattie, as if surprised. 'But so unfortunate.'

'I don't understand.' Mattie had decided to get her own oar into the conversation. Meriam was about five foot nine, slim, well proportioned, with the tribal markings on her forehead. But charming. Two big dimples dotted her cheeks, and her white teeth shone from her black face.

'I, too,' Meriam continued. 'But I have no man, you must understand.'

'I don't,' laughed Mattie. 'I don't understand, that is.'

'The custom,' Meriam explained. 'Watch your stepping—footing? There is a ditch here. Well, now, a woman—a young woman raised in her father's house—has a youth name. Like me—Meriam. When I choose a man, then I will no longer be called Meriam, but rather Metchak's woman—or whatever the man's name may be. But when I have my first male child, *then* I receive my lifetime name. I will be known as Cheda's mother—Cheda, that's the name I have selected for my first son. So you are Mattie. But you should be known as Latimore's woman.' She had led them through the crowd as she spoke, and a path opened in front of her without command.

'And so much for women's liberation,' Ryan whispered in Mattie's ear.

'Explain to her,' Mattie whispered fiercely. '*I'm* the Latimore, not you!'

'What? And start a riot in the middle of this crowd? Just remember, Latimore's woman, this whole thing was your idea!'

'Oh, you——!' Mattie was about to put him in his place when two tall Masakin Tiwal came up behind her, one on each side, and grabbed her upper arms. A similar pair took Ryan under their hands. She was too frightened to say another word. Meriam, seeing the look on her face, rescued her.

'There is nothing to fear,' she said softly. 'The Chief is receiving ambassadors from other tribes. As representatives of the Latimore clan you will be received, but only at the end of the list, you understand. We do not know this Latimore people. The guards are a formality. Nobody may approach the Chief with hands free. It is the custom.'

'Ryan, I'm scared,' Mattie blurted out.

'No need to worry,' he soothed. 'I'll take care of you.'

'Sure you will,' she returned through chattering teeth. 'There's one of you and fifteen thousand of them.'

'You're exaggerating,' he chuckled. 'There can't be more than five or six thousand right here. That's considerably better odds.'

'You should have brought the rifle,' she snapped. 'At least that would give us a chance!'

'Hardly,' he returned. 'I don't have any shells. Come on now, Mattie, buck up.'

'Yeah, buck up,' she said angrily. 'It's easy for you to say! Find something that'll make me feel better, or shut up!'

'How about this?' he chuckled. 'Mattie Latimore, I love you!'

Her head whirled round so suddenly that her hat flew off. She stared up at him with eyes as big as saucers, eyes filling rapidly with tears.

'Oh, dear,' he muttered, 'I didn't think you'd find it all *that* distasteful!'

'Just because I'm scared to death and a long way from home—it doesn't help for you to lie to me, Ryan!'

'Lie to you?' he echoed. Everyone in the vicinity turned to stare at him. 'I'm not lying to you, Mattie,' he said more softly. 'Meriam, tell these gorillas to turn me loose so I can prove it!'

The Masakin girl giggled at them both. 'It is not possible,' she said. 'Once the ceremony has begun, it is not possible. You both look—ah, my language fails me. There is much I cannot say in English. I studied at the Christian College in Juba, and there were many words the missionaries did not teach.'

'Your English is perfect,' Mattie said determinedly. 'Only he *lies* a lot!'

'What man does not,' Meriam said casually, 'when he seeks the woman he wants?' It all sounds so simple, Mattie thought. Philosophy in Darkest Africa? And yet the girl sounds so sure of herself. She can hardly be—sixteen, perhaps? Why should she know so much more about—things—than I do?

'And now is your turn,' Meriam told them softly. 'Walk with the warriors. Do not make any movements. Stand straight and tall. Bow the head when the chief acknowledges. What do you want me to say to him for you?'

'Say to him?' Ryan fumbled through his list of clichés. It was obvious, from watching the ambassadors preceding him, that the greetings were a formality, nothing more. 'Say to the Chief that the House of Latimore brings greetings and friendship from across the Great Water.'

'Wow!' the Masakin girl giggled. 'You mean from the United States? What part? We studied much geography in my school.'

'Texas,' muttered Ryan.

'That ought to teach you to spout off, Mr Livingstone,' Mattie whispered. 'Across the Great Water! Good lord, there's a lot of ham in you, Ryan Quinn!'

'Texas,' mused Meriam. 'A big land, Texas. Many cattle!'

There was no place for further conversation. Their guards began to advance them in route step down the narrow path that led to the presentation point. As they walked slowly, Mattie concentrated on the figure in front of them. The Chief was a Masakin Tiwal, the tall tribe. He lazed on a wooden throne, set on a dais that elevated him a couple of feet above the ground. His height and the added height of the throne made him look tremendously tall. A thin man, well scarred, he wore a feathered headpiece that added to his imperial dignity, and nothing else. It was impossible to judge his age. At his feet sat a comfortably large woman, adorned with the tribal scars, whose keen eyes darted this way and that, as if she were the major-domo of the meeting.

As they waited in line behind two others to be presented, Ryan said, 'How come they don't hold *your* hands, Meriam?'

'Me?' the girl said under her breath. 'Why should they? I am the daughter of the Chief. Remember, don't say a word!'

'But I speak a few words of Masakin,' he protested.

'Do what the lady says,' Mattie muttered at him. 'Shut up, Ryan!'

'You *do* love to give orders, don't you?' he returned stubbornly.

'Hush,' Meriam interrupted. 'Now it's my turn.' The young girl stepped out in front of them, and in a loud voice began a statement in Masakin. The Chief, who had looked a little sleepy, sat up straight in his chair. The woman at his feet smiled, a broad, eager smile that held some hidden meaning.

'What's she saying?' Mattie whispered to Ryan.

'Talk about puffing us up!' he whispered. 'She's saying something about the Latimore clan who come from the wide lands of Texas, the land of many cattle. And then she's adding a few lies about how big our cattle land is, and how we've come all this way to acknowledge the Chief Artafi Masakin!'

It must have been a fine harangue, Mattie told herself. The Chief actually waved a hand in acknowledgement, and the woman at his feet clapped her hands twice, a move that was instantly taken up by the crowd. But their part of the ceremony was over. As the clapping subsided, their warrior escorts locked on to their arms and took them away into the crowd at a dog-trot.

Once out of the crowd, the warriors turned them loose, as if they had lost all interest, and disappeared into the crowd. An older man appeared and whispered a few words in Meriam's ear. The girl laughed.

'What?' Ryan asked anxiously.

'The presentation was a great success,' the girl said. 'I was supposed to show you a camping area above the village. Now my mother commands you to have a hut in the Chief's compound. And you—Mattie?—my mother will receive you among the women in her hut tonight!'

'Oh, brother,' sighed Ryan. 'Well, I warned you, Cinderella. And now you have an audience with the Queen!'

'Great heavens!' Mattie moaned. 'What will I say?'

'Not to worry,' he advised. Angrily, she kicked a cloud of dust at him.

'Not to worry?' she echoed tautly. 'Not to worry? *You* can say that! Well, darn you, Ryan Quinn, I'll worry if I *want* to!'

CHAPTER EIGHT

'HOW DO I look?' Mattie twirled around in front of Ryan. Her skirt and blouse, which had disappeared from their hut at noon, just after the reception, had reappeared at dusk, washed to perfection, and neatly folded.

'Nice enough to eat,' Ryan commented, sitting crosslegged on the hard-packed floor. 'You're bound to knock 'em dead. Nervous?'

'Scared to death,' she confessed. 'What can I *say*?'

'Hell, I don't know,' he grumbled. 'About the only way we could get their help is if they owned the railroad.'

Owned the railroad? The thought rambled around in Mattie's brain, looking for a place to settle. *If they owned the railroad!* 'But the railroad belongs to the government,' she said softly, feeling for an idea.

'Yeah,' he retorted. 'But the government also says it owns all the land, and that doesn't stop people who want to use it! Do that whirl-around thing again. I like to see that.'

She grinned at his challenge. 'You mean, like this?' Up on tiptoe she went, whirled around twice and thought, this is the only profit I've ever got from all those ballet lessons Ma made me take. I'll bet I can do it twice more.

And that, of course, put the gypsy curse on things. On the third twirl her foot slipped. She teetered for a second, vainly trying to regain her balance, then fell over, right into Ryan's lap. Her skirt flew up as she landed, exposing more than a little of her long, slim legs.

135

'Well, now,' he said, and gave her that patented leer of his. 'Pennies from heaven!'

'Don't be a fool,' she gasped, completely out of breath. She started to get up, but his arm came around and held her as in a vice. His dark eyes, too close for comfort, searched her face and then prodded at the sprawling length of her. Anxiously she tried to adjust the hem of her skirt. There was a moment of struggle within her and then, as if only a *pro forma* protest was needed, she relaxed and settled back in his arms.

'I don't understand you,' he murmured. 'I thought I did—all women, for that matter. I see the outside of you, but I have no idea what goes on inside that head of yours.'

'I don't seem to understand me either,' she sighed. 'I always have, you know. I had my life planned out—ever since I was thirteen. There wasn't any place in it for someone named Ryan Quinn. No place. What have you done to me?'

'That's my question,' he growled. 'What the hell have you done to *me*?'

'Did you mean that, what you said out on the field?'

'What did I say?'

'You said—I——' She was too embarrassed to repeat it. If he couldn't remember, he couldn't have meant it, could he? It was just another one of those little white lies. Something to give her a little courage! She glued her lips together.

'If you mean *I love you*,' he whispered, 'I meant every word of it at the time.'

'At the time, huh? You mean back then, but not now?'

'Time to go.' Meriam walked in through the open doorway. She stopped short just inside. 'Oh!' she gasped. 'I did not mean to interrupt! Please excuse me!'

'You didn't interrupt a thing,' Mattie said bitterly as she pushed away from Ryan and came up to her feet. 'Not a thing. My—er—man here was suffering from hoof-in-mouth disease. I'm ready.'

'That sounds terrible,' the young Masakin girl said worriedly. 'Do the cattle get sick from this?'

'Never,' Mattie answered. 'It only affects men.'

Behind them as they walked away she could hear Ryan gargling in his throat, as if he were trying to swallow some very nasty words indeed. Just the thought gave Mattie a little glow of satisfaction.

Torches lit the centre of the village. Meriam led her by the hand to the smaller of two structures, completely different from the towered huts. A long, low building with a high, thatched roof, almost fifty feet long, was their target.

'That one is the men's council house.' Meriam pointed to the other building, which stretched a good hundred feet into the darkness. 'Duck your head. This entrance is low—to emphasise humility, it is said.'

'The women never go in the other council building?' Mattie asked.

'Never. Come.' They were in an small outer compartment. The doorway in front of them was covered by a hanging linen sheet. It was the first covered doorway Mattie had ever seen in these Masakin villages. All the others were open to the night air—and visitors. Two very elderly women sat on either side of it, almost as guards. Both of them were puffing on tiny pipes. Meriam stopped just long enough to take off her blouse, and, without looking back at Mattie, led the way by the linen barrier.

Inside the air was warm. A curtain of smoke lay up in the high eaves. The entire room was crowded with women of all sizes and shapes, most sucking at their pipes. A tiny dung fire glowed in the centre of an open space. On the far side, ensconced on a bed of pillows, was the same large, graceful woman who had been sitting at the Chief's feet during the reception ceremony. 'Come,' Meriam urged. 'Do what I do.' Her hand came back. Mattie grabbed it and followed.

As they passed around the fire in front of this huge, inspecting audience, Mattie could feel an embarrassed blush rise to her cheeks. A hissing murmur came from the crowd. It sounded like disapproval. Meriam came to a dead stop about four paces from the Chief's wife, fell to her knees, and bowed her head. Mattie followed clumsily. She was agile enough, but sitting on her bent feet had never been common practice. The bow was easy. She *wanted* to avoid those penetrating eyes. After a moment of silence Meriam said something quickly in the Masakin tongue. Another moment of silence, and the Chief's wife answered—something short, sharp, pithy. The audience stirred.

Meriam turned around to look at Mattie. 'It is my fault,' the girl said. 'I should have noticed. The Great One says, why do you come before her to insult her, wearing clothes to cover your heart?'

'You mean I——'

'Look around you,' Meriam advised. Every woman in the hut, and there must have been over a hundred, was naked.

'You mean I have to take—everything?'

'Not everything,' Meriam said sympathetically. 'As I have done. She must see your heart.'

'Great gobs of goose-grease,' Mattie sighed. 'Well, I suppose—they're all women?'

'All women.'

'Tell the—er—the Great One it was ignorance, and not intention,' Mattie said quietly as her fingers busied themselves with her buttons. She had forgotten her camisole. Under the blouse she wore—nothing. As it slid off over her head there was another sigh that seemed to run completely around the room. Mattie slumped back down on her heels, straightened her shoulders, and looked straight into the eyes of the Chief's wife. The woman searched her face for a moment, nodded, then said something. Mattie could hear the sympathy in her tone, the kindness in her expression, and felt relieved. Until the words came.

'The Great One says,' Meriam translated, 'that she did not realise that the Latimore woman was white all over. Had she known, she would never have required you to display your ugliness to all. She begs you to overlook. Should you desire, you may put on your blouse again.'

'No.' Mattie straightened up. 'One must see the heart to hear the truth.'

'How clever you are,' Meriam whispered. 'Do you know the ritual?'

Mattie shook her head. The Masakin girl turned to translate. A big smile spread across the face of the Chief's wife, and a scattering of applause spread throughout the room. One score for the Latimore tribe, Mattie told herself, drawing a mental figure in the air. The Chief's wife spoke again, gesturing. Heads nodded agreement throughout the room. Meriam paused for a moment, as if seeking the right words.

'The Great One now says we speak informally,' she translated. 'I am to say—my mother speaks of the power of the Latimore tribe. She has seen the camp at Kosti. There are many strong men, and a—thousand machines to make them more powerful.' The girl paused for another second. 'Numbers are hard,' she confessed. 'We do not have a word for numbers bigger than one hundred. You will understand? She asks me to write the name of your tribe so all can see—in English.'

Mattie sank back on her heels again, a smile on her gamine face. See, it isn't all that hard, after all, she thought. The smile expanded into a grin. The Latimore tribe is in high repute? So maybe I should gild the lily? Meriam was using a stick to draw the Latimore name in large size in the hard-packed floor. Heads craned all around the room as the girl came back beside Mattie.

'Your mother thinks the Kosti camp is big?' Mattie asked cautiously.

'Yes. Very big. My mother has not travelled much. Is there something wrong?'

'Not exactly. Actually, the Kosti camp is one of the smallest the Latimore tribe has. We have eighty-nine other camps all over the world, all bigger than the one at Kosti.'

'This is true?' Meriam asked.

'Cross my heart,' chuckled Mattie, and made the universal gesture. Meriam turned around and began talking. The room became silent—very silent. The Chief's wife stood up and took a pace forwards.

'My mother asks, are there many machines?'

'Thousands,' Mattie assured her.

'I can't say that,' Meriam objected. 'Suppose—like the stars in the sky?'

'Like the stars in the sky,' Mattie agreed. The girl began translating at high speed. It took a surprising number of words to express such a little. Meriam's padding her part, Mattie thought immediately.

When she stopped translating, her mother began a speech. It took minutes, and Meriam looked puzzled.

'My mother says——' The girl fumbled for a moment. 'Once, we were a great power. Masakin chiefs sat on the throne of the Pharaohs. We were driven from our lands

four times. The Chiefs of long ago decided to withdraw
here, to Nuba. To keep our culture as it has been. My
mother says—this council meets to decide if that was a
mistake. If we should not go forward, like the Nuer, and
gain machines, and rule again as we properly should. If
we do not, we will be crushed, and disappear into the
wind, like the leaves that fall from the trees.'

Silence. It hung in the air like the smoke, a miasma
of thought hanging over the packed women. Some were
uneasy. Some of the younger ones smiled and nodded.
The rest sat silent. The Chief's wife broke it with another
question.

'My mother says you are to state your position in the
Latimore tribe, and that of your man.'

Change of subject, Mattie told herself. Big principles
followed by little thoughts. What is my position? And
that of my man? They'd have a fit if they knew! But
I'm entitled to bragging rights!

She stood up. She and the Chief's wife were the only
ones standing. 'Tell your mother that I am the daughter
of the house,' Mattie said. Meriam gasped. Well, it's
almost true, Mattie told herself. I'm one of the *four*
daughters of the house, but surely I can fudge a little,
this far away?

'That word,' Meriam said slowly. 'I do not understand—daughter of the house?'

'It means—well, my father is the Chief Latimore, you
understand. The Chief of the tribe. I am his daughter.'
Meriam grinned from ear to ear, and tried out the phrase
a couple of times. 'Daughter of the house? As I am,
Latimore woman. I am the daughter of the Masakin
house!' She clapped her hands and made a rapid trans-
lation. A susurration of sound swept around the audience. The Chief's wife moved to one side, and made a
gesture.

'My mother says you are welcome many times, and you are invited to sit with her in recognition of your dignity.'

Me? Mattie thought. My dignity? I'm sitting here half naked thousands of miles from home, and I've got dignity? And another thought followed quickly on the first. Of course I have. They all have. They don't need clothes or possessions to have dignity!

Sitting beside the Chief's wife was something different from being isolated in the middle of a conference, like a bug under a scientist's microscope. Reality was beginning to fade. The faces around her became faint and far away. Meriam's voice disappeared, and it was almost as if she could converse directly with the Great One.

'So,' that lady said, 'you do not understand? Listen. My great-ancestor was Pharaoh in Egypt. His daughter was his heir. Only by marrying Pharaoh's daughter could another man become leader, and it is still so with us. My father was Chief. Artafi Chief because I chose him—I married him. My sons will not be Chiefs. The husband my daughter chooses will succeed Artafi. Now you see?'

Marry the boss's daughter, Mattie told herself. Is that what Ryan is up to? There was a sick feeling in her stomach. Without thinking, she took the cup that Meriam offered, and drained off the strong drink.

'It is too bad you are so ugly,' the Chief's wife mused. 'The colour—it must be an embarrassment to you?'

'I try to hide it,' Mattie smiled as she accepted another full cup.

'It is too late to do much, but there is *something* we can do. We can give you the heart sign!'

'What in the world is that?' Mattie asked Meriam. The young girl turned around.

'See—on my shoulder,' she said. Mattie stared. High on her left shoulder was a line of cicatrices, circular scars. 'The sign of our tribe,' Meriam explained. 'Over the heart, to mark commitment.'

'Hey, I don't want to be punctured!' Mattie protested, drinking down her bowl's contents.

'Not punctured,' Meriam squealed in glee. 'You are too old for that. It is what you call—tattoo? Is that the right word?'

'Tattoo. I don't mind a little tattoo,' Mattie agreed, owl-eyed. 'Will it help?'

'It will make you a member of *our* house,' Meriam smiled. 'Yes?'

'Why not?' said Mattie, loaded with false courage.

'But you do not tell us about your man,' Meriam's mother insisted. 'He will be Latimore Chief when your father dies?'

Mattie struggled to get her thoughts in proper order. One miscue would knock down all the edifice she had managed to build. Would Ryan marry her to be head of the Latimore empire? What a laugh that would be! Michael was the designated heir!

'It is not yet settled,' she said shyly. 'My man is from— Texas. He owns many cattle—one hundred hundreds.'

'Ah.' The black matron beside her nodded, no longer Chief's wife, but mother. 'The bride price is not settled. I can see it would be difficult between two such great tribes. Meriam, give our guest another drink!'

The women's conference went on for five hours, into the depths of the night, and then they called the doctor. When Mattie came to, she was sitting on a bare table in another little round hut, away from the camp. A wrinkled old man stood at her side, smiling a toothless smile. A worried Meriam was standing at his side.

'You were sick,' the girl explained. 'Everybody laughed. You drank much beer. This is Mashoto. He is—a doctor.'

'Good lord!' Mattie exclaimed. 'A real witch-doctor?'

'Not exactly,' the old man said in perfect English. 'I trained in Cairo. But I am not insulted. My father was a witch-doctor, and I think perhaps he knew more about medicine than me. Now, they are making you beautiful, eh? We will put a little alcohol on that just to make sure. Lovely design.' Mattie suddenly realised how truly naked she was, and her hands flew up to cover her breasts. The doctor laughed.

'I have also pumped your stomach. You feel better?'

'Oh, my!' Mattie sighed. 'I made a mess of it, did I?'

'No mess,' Meriam assured her. 'It was very entertaining. Everyone comments. My mother is proud to know you. She will talk with you again tomorrow—just you.'

There was a sudden noise in the background—a crackling sound, and a voice. The doctor shrugged and walked over into the corner, carrying a flare with him.

'What's that?' asked Mattie, half knowing the answer already.

'The bush telegraph,' the doctor chuckled. Looking over his shoulder, Mattie could see the Panasonic label on the little battery-powered radio transmitter.

'Now you go back to your man,' the doctor advised. 'Rest, sleep. Tomorrow you may have headache. Your shoulder might be just a little sore. Take two aspirins. No excitement.' He gave her a little bottle of pills, and helped her down off the table. With Meriam's help, she managed it down the hill and into the hut assigned to her Latimore man.

*   *   *

Slowly, carefully, Mattie pried one eye open. She was lying flat on her back inside the bedroll. The hut was crowded. Six or seven woman, looking to be from sixteen to sixty, were gathered around her, giggling. Mattie tried the other eye. It was plastered shut. She turned her head to see better, and regretted it instantly.

'Head bother you, does it?' Ryan remarked from behind her. She knew better the second time. Instead of turning to look, she let her head sink gradually back on to the little pillow-roll.

'Aspirin,' she moaned. 'Oh, lord, what did I——'

'You tied one on,' he chuckled.

'Don't talk so loudly,' she groaned. 'Aspirin—the doctor gave me some aspirin. I don't understand——'

'That was millet beer,' he told her. 'Half the senior women in camp are under the weather. Here, try this.'

He dropped two tablets into her hand, then held her head up gently, while holding a cup of cold tea to her mouth. She sipped first, then swallowed. 'I thought it was—I don't know what I thought it was,' she grumbled.

'Let's hope a hangover is all you've got. They don't pasteurise beer in these parts.'

'You don't have to be so pleased about it,' she complained. 'What are all these—these people doing here?'

'They came to see,' he explained. 'The word is out all over the festival camp that you're white all over! They came to see!'

'Oh, heavens!' she whispered. 'Get them out of here!' In her anger, she forgot her condition, and sat up. Her head spun. There was an instantaneous shriek of pleasure from the watching women, who ran for the door as Ryan made shooing motions. Both hands went up to keep her head from falling off.

'You know, they're right,' said Ryan. He was trying to sound solemn, but she could hear the laughter running through the words. 'You *are* white all over!'

Forgetting her head, Mattie looked down at herself, sitting up in a fold of the old bedroll. For a moment her mind refused to grasp what she saw—acres and acres of Mattie Latimore, all on public view! She dropped back on her pillow and pulled up the blanket. The pain in her head brought tears to her eyes.

'Where the devil are my clothes?' she muttered angrily through the tears.

Ryan came over to the bed and slipped one arm under her, cuddling her against his side. 'Cry it out, love,' he sighed. 'I know I shouldn't pick on you like I did. Put it down to inexperience.'

'If I had the strength,' she wailed angrily, 'I'd put *you* down, you—— Who took my clothes off me?'

'Would you believe—Meriam?' he asked solicitously.

'No, I wouldn't!'

'Well, then, I won't have to tell you a lie. I did it. I chopped down the cherry tree with my own little hatchet.'

'Why, you rotten——'

'Now, now, Mattie,' he cautioned, 'don't say that. I have it on good repute that my mother and father were married when I was born.'

'I'm sorry,' she muttered as she snuggled closer to his shirt. Ryan grinned down at her, but said nothing. Moments later he shifted, so her head was lying in his lap. She coiled herself up, glad of the support, happy to be close to him. The aspirins were working their magic. She could almost reason logically. Almost.

Why am I so glad to be where I am? she asked herself. Why does it hurt, and yet feel so nice? Why don't I really care that he undressed me without my knowledge? Because, her conscience intervened, you love him. But I

don't want to love him, she thought sadly. I don't really
know him. He's bound to Virginia in some unholy
manner. After all, what have we had together? A couple
of kisses, a wild night of skinny-dipping, and eight quiet,
restful days in an oxcart. That makes a romance? Even
a poor primitive like Meriam's mother knows what he's
up to. He wants a share of the Latimore empire! Doesn't
he?

'You know,' she said hesitantly, 'I don't have any
money of my own except for my salary.'

'Is that a fact?' he drawled. 'I would have thought
you'd be worth a bucket of bucks. Don't you own any
part of Latimore?'

'Yes, of course I do. All of us have a share, but all
my profits go into a blind trust and are given away to
charity at the end of each year. I don't even get to say
which charity!'

'Well, how about that?' he returned. And never have
I heard anyone less interested, Mattie thought. Is that a
good sign, or is he just a consummate actor?

'And when my brother Michael's twenty-one I won't
even have the vice-president's job,' she hurried on.

'Good for Michael,' he commented, bored. 'I wish I
knew what this council is all about. Just a hint, so I
could lay on some pitch about the railroad.'

'You're not very interested in me,' she objected. 'In
another few years I won't have a rag for my back.'

'You don't have one now.' Ryan laughed, pulling back
the edge of her blanket and peering down at her. 'And
I'm interested as hell!'

'Oh, you!' Mattie slapped at his hand and pulled her
protection back in place. 'Men! You're all alike!'

'I believe so,' he drawled. 'Why are you trying to pick
a fight with me?'

'I'm—not,' she stammered. 'I just—I know what the council is up to.'

He grinned down at her, and used one hand to brush her hair out of her face. 'Sure you do. They told you all about it in the women's meeting last night.'

'You're darn right,' Mattie flared at him. 'You see everything around this camp, but you haven't the slightest idea what's going on! A typical male attitude!'

'But you're going to put me straight, right?'

'I really ought to slap your silly face,' she snapped, struggling to sit up. His arm restrained her, then turned her loose, and she squirmed around to face him. 'Now listen!' she said furiously. 'The council has one major issue in front of them. Are you listening? Look at me when I talk to you!'

'I'm looking,' he sighed. 'And my eyeballs are about to fall out!'

Mattie angrily followed the direction of his eyes and immediately turned red. One of her *gallabiyas* was lying across the foot of the bed. She came up on her knees, back to him, and snatched up the long white gown.

'Need some help?'

'Not yours,' she muttered. 'Peeping Tom!' She ducked her head into the dress, and started to pull it over her shoulders, when his hands halted the movement.

'Look at that!' he exclaimed. 'What happened to your shoulder?'

The utter stupidity of her entire reaction hit Mattie in the stomach. She settled back on her haunches, working the gown over her head and down around her hips. It was almost impossible not to laugh.

'That's my beauty treatment,' she said proudly. 'The Chief's wife was so startled that I was so ugly—that she had her people give me a beauty mark. I needed it!'

Ryan pulled the *gallabiya* off her shoulder and studied the design. 'Looks almost like hieroglyphics. I don't know about the beauty part of it—you were beautiful enough before.'

'It's the tribal insignia,' she explained. 'They adopted me into the Masakin. And there's a lot you don't know. None of this is what you think. The Chief hasn't a whole lot to say about things. The members of the council are elected, and the Chief can only do what the consensus of the council turns out to be. And they're facing the biggest decision they've had to make in hundreds of years.'

'Tell, oh fount of knowledge,' said Ryan in graceful Arabic. Mattie stuck her tongue out at him.

'Nobody likes a smart aleck,' she informed him primly. 'That's my father's favourite saying. For your information, the Masakin are deciding at this council whether to keep to the old tribal ways, or to convert to modern life and machinery, as the Nuer tribes have done.'

'Holy cats!' he exclaimed. She shushed him, to no effect. A few more visitors put their heads around the corner of the doorway to look.

'This meeting is at the fourth hour,' said Ryan, checking his watch. 'Ten o'clock. In about half an hour. I don't think I'll be able to get a word in edgewise, not if the problem is *that* serious. What would you suggest?'

'And isn't that a surprise,' said Mattie smugly. 'The great Ryan Quinn *asking*!'

'Well, we agreed we were equal partners. Almost!'

'Your ego is insufferably huge,' she snapped.

'And just matches yours,' he laughed. 'No wonder we make a great team!'

We do, don't we? she thought, and the sunny grin escaped her control. 'I have a suggestion, but no questions asked,' she said.

'No questions,' he promised. Look at that, she scolded at herself. Have you ever seen a man who looked more trusting, more trustworthy, more handsome, more daring, more—— Yeah, sure, her conscience interrupted. And he lies a lot!

'When you go into this meeting, look for a moment to make a simple statement. Just say, ''How would you like to run a railroad?'' Don't add anything, don't pad the part. Just that.'

'That's a wicked gleam you have in your eye,' he told her. 'All right, I'll do it. I have to go now. How about a kiss for good luck?'

'For the corporation's sake,' she qualified, lying without fear for her mortal soul. He came at her like a leopard at the kill, and before she could get her lips half shut he was upon them, plundering her mouth with gentle passion. What have I been missing all these years? she thought breathlessly, and threw herself into the ravaging with a happy heart.

In a land where the clock runs at the dictates of the people instead of the other way around, it was hard to measure that kiss. Lack of air brought it to an end. Mattie lay back in Ryan's arms, aware that one of his hands was cupping her breast through the thin cotton of the *gallabiya*, and not caring. Or perhaps that was said wrong. She cared, but did not object. Mattie Latimore had cast her lot with Ryan Quinn, and would think of the consequences some other day.

'That was—fairly interesting, for a novice,' he drawled. He was as breathless as she. Fire burned in his dark eyes, and Mattie knew full well who would be burned by it.

'Do you like children?' he asked, completely out of the blue. And, not waiting for her answer, 'I've got to get going. How about a kiss for luck?'

'I love children,' she gasped, 'and there seems to be an echo in here. You just did that bit.'

'What bit?'

'The part about kissing for good luck!'

'I *am* forgetful,' he sighed. 'I need someone to look after me. What are you going to be doing while I'm away?'

'I have another meeting with the Chief's wife,' Mattie said. It was difficult to speak at all. It required all her attention to stare into his eyes. He wasn't blinking, and the old New England superstition was if you can out-blink your opponent you were sure to be lucky. And I do so want to be lucky, she told herself.

She might have won the contest had Ryan been fair—but he had no inclination towards fairness. While she stared, his head came closer and closer, until her will-power failed her and she closed her eyes. Once again came that assault. His warm lips on hers, plundering her mouth, his hand gently palpitating her soft breast. It was not a moment of conquest. Mattie did her part. Her mouth met his in combat, her arms seized on the nape of his neck and pressed him harder to the task, and all the time she squirmed in his direction, trying to get closer, trying to transmit by osmosis what she had not the courage to put into words.

There was a clatter of noise at the door. 'The council begins,' Meriam announced as she walked in, 'and the Great One waits for you, Latimore's woman! Oops—I have done it again?'

Latimore's woman prised herself out of his arms and grinned at them both. 'No, not at all, Meriam,' she called happily. 'I was just coming.'

CHAPTER NINE

MATTIE waited around all day for Ryan to return. There was a quiet cloud hanging over the village. People sat around in small groups, watching the council hut. It rained and stopped and rained again, and no one paid it any attention. As for *her* part in their little scheme, it was ridiculously easy. Meriam had conducted her to her mother's hut, high on the hill near the doctor. There had been no formality; everything was business.

'Anyone can learn to run a railroad,' she assured the Chief's wife in response to half a dozen rapid-fire questions. 'Look at the Nuer tribe. Ten years ago they knew only cattle; now they dig for oil, drive trucks, everything. The Masakin can do the same. Latimore will establish a school and provide the training at our base in Kosti. While we train the men we will need guards for the track system. Let us say one hundred men to train, two hundred men to guard. And we can build cattle crossings, so your herds can pass over. Is it possible?'

'Anything is possible,' the woman answered. 'There are five one hundred hundreds of Masakin.'

'And you can get the men to do this?'

Meriam's mother laughed. 'You have much to learn, Latimore woman. Men cannot be commanded—but they *can* be convinced. That is a woman's job. Tonight the council will smoke a pipe and sleep on their words. They will have dreams. Tomorrow they will be convinced.'

'Wow!' laughed Mattie. 'I've got to get some of your tobacco.'

'Not tobacco,' the Chief's wife admitted. 'Here—look. You know it?'

'Oh, my!' Mattie exclaimed, suddenly sobered. 'Hashish!'

'Just so,' the older woman said. 'Sometimes we find purpose in Arab gifts. The Chief will smoke his pipe and lie down. No one but his wife may join him. The same with the other men. Words will be whispered in their ears—how else are dreams made? It is a bitter thing to do. We Masakin women interfere only at terrible times— this is one. Our people must either change, or disappear. Now you go. Tomorrow I fix this thing with you and your man. I don't understand your mother, letting you live with him and he has not paid the bride-price! You Latimores have strange customs!'

Ryan came back just at sunset, exhausted. 'Hardest work I ever did,' he complained. 'Sitting there listening.'

'But you did get your lines in?' Mattie asked anxiously.

'Indeed I did,' he chuckled. 'I never realised how great an actor I am. Your father ought to double my salary.'

'At least that,' she muttered, going about the business of assembling a meal.

He came up behind her and put his arms around her. 'I don't mean that,' he said softly. 'My contract is up in ten more days, and I don't intend to renew it.'

She turned around, flustered. 'But—but then we——'

'But *then we* is right,' he interrupted. 'We're going to get this deal working, and then we're going to pay attention strictly to *and then we*. Incidentally, I've had nothing but repetitions today. They think I own a thousand cattle, and every one of them kept shaking their heads, telling me I should never have let that information get out, because it would increase the price! I wish I knew what they were talking about.'

Mattie piled up their communal plate. Rice and vegetables as before, but this time including savoury bits of beef. 'You and I have to have a serious talk,' she told him. 'Try this.'

'Hmm, good,' he said after a few samples. 'Real meat. Oh, I was getting sick of that vegetarian diet!'

'But it was healthy,' she said firmly.

'Yeah, healthy,' he agreed drily. 'Now, what was it you wanted to talk about?'

She went at it cautiously. 'The Chief's wife,' she started out, 'felt that we made a nice couple.'

'Uh-huh. And then what?'

'And then she asked me how much you paid for me, and I didn't have an answer.' She looked over at him, all meekness and primness. 'I suppose a girl ought to know what she's worth.'

'So?'

'And then she felt badly about it because my mother should never have let me live with you without—well, you know.'

'You sound like a girl about to tell me something I don't want to hear.' Ryan managed a smile as he reached for his tea to wash the dinner down.

Oh, lord, Mattie thought, I've blown the works!

'The word that's choking you,' he added, 'is *marriage*, right?'

'I—yes——' she stammered. 'That word has come up a time or two.'

'And what do you think about it?'

'The word?' she mumbled.

'The deed,' he laughed.

'I—what do *you* think about it?'

'Well——' Ryan finished off his share of the meal, rinsed his hands in the water bucket, and settled back against the wall of the hut. 'Considering everything? You don't have any money, you said, and you'll lose your job when brother Michael comes of age. On the other hand, you're a fairly good engineer, a fair manager, and you *might* be a good architect if you work hard at it. Then again, I'm figuring to settle down, I've got a lot more than a thousand head of cattle on my ranch back in Texas, you're a nice-looking little thing, and when you walk around here wiggling that cute little bottom I always seem to have this insane urge to jump on you——'

'Well!' she snapped indignantly.

'Don't interrupt,' he said calmly. 'It's one of those bad habits you're going to have to correct. Where was I? Oh, yeah, you're one hell of a fun girl to go oxcart riding with. That eight days to Topari changed my thinking completely. And there's one more little item. I think I'm top over tea-kettle in love with you. Now you can talk.'

Mattie's glare started to fade, changed into a blush, then was surmounted by a wide smile. 'You don't seem to have left me anything to say,' she stammered.

'That's the way it's supposed to be,' he teased. 'All you have to say is yes. Y-e-s. Have you got that?'

'Yes,' she sighed, 'I've got that. Yes. Do I click my heels and bow?'

Ryan ducked away from the fire, laughing. 'Put that plate down, Mattie—it's the only one we own! We won't be able to eat if you throw it at me! It was a joke!'

'Yeah, joke,' she snapped. 'Funny! That kind of humour will get you a lot of nights sleeping on the sofa. They'll get you tomorrow!'

'They?' he queried.

'My fellow tribespeople. Why do you think they inducted me into the Masakin tribe? So I could have some family for you to bargain with, dummy!'

'A manager's day is never done,' he sighed. 'Come over here, woman.'

She came. Reluctantly, but she came. Not ready to haul down her flag, but willing at least to stop disputing the passage. Ryan put one arm casually around her. A gaggle of children raced past their doorway and laughed at them. The darkness closed in as more fires were lit throughout the village. A happy stillness came upon both of them as, in two separate bodies, they dreamed the same dream.

It lasted until the fourth hour of the night, sounded on a gazelle horn bugle. The council was still debating. 'Time to get to bed,' announced Ryan. They stood up simultaneously and went arm-in-arm into the sleeping hut.

'Now we're engaged?' he asked.

'I don't see any sign of it,' Mattie returned softly. He fumbled with the signet ring on his little finger, and pushed it on to her left hand. It hung there, too large for her long, slim fingers. '*Now* we're engaged,' he announced.

'OK.'

'That's it? OK?'

'I—think so,' she said. 'I have this—sort of suspicion about you whenever you make statements like that. What comes after the *now we're engaged*?'

'I thought that was obvious,' he chuckled. 'Now, when we share the same sleeping-bag, we can consider other things besides sleeping.'

'Oh, no, we can't!' Mattie backed away from him, both hands raised in front of her.

'Now what did I do wrong?'

'Nothing—yet,' she sighed. 'Look, Ryan. You've been away from home a long time, so I *have* to tell you. The sexual revolution in America is over.'

She had expected a volcanic explosion. Instead, he studied her solemn face for a moment and smiled. 'OK, lady,' he said.

'You *do* see, don't you?' she sighed. 'I knew you would.'

'And that's what I get for tonight,' he said wryly. 'And a little kiss?'

'Little is the operative word,' she said primly.

The following day started with a burst of sunshine. Smoke rose from the council house. Meriam came by in the first hour, laughing. 'The council has reached a decision,' she announced. 'They will tell it at the sixth hour. And the matchmakers are waiting for you, Latimore man!'

'Waiting for me?' Ryan gave a good impression of a man who had no idea what she was talking about. Mattie stretched and came out of the sleeping-bag. Ryan sat up in the middle of the two borrowed blankets he had used as a bed, in the opposite corner.

'Time to put your money where your mouth is, high roller,' Mattie teased. 'I'm coming along to make sure the game isn't fixed.'

'Oh, no,' said Meriam solemnly, 'never that. You are not allowed to hear the—discussion.'

So the two of them walked off, talking happily, leaving Mattie all alone. 'I'm being auctioned off,' she muttered as she went around the hut, picking things up, 'and I don't even get to listen? Some system. But it doesn't bother me!'

And it didn't, of course. Why would a modern woman worry about something like that? It had nothing to do with her floor-pacing, or her dash up to the top of the hill, 'To get some air,' she told herself. Down below her in the village, the councillors were wandering out of the council house, yawning, scratching, congratulating each other. Just outside the village, in the shade of a tree, the bargaining team was gathered in a circle, laughing, speech-making, and generally having a good time. 'Stupid customs,' Mattie told the Egyptian vulture over head, but her pretence could not prevent her legs from carrying her down the hill in a large spiral, closer and closer to the tree.

There was a big cheer from the bargainers before she arrived, and a similarly big cheer for the councillors on the other side of the square. But nobody wanted to talk to Mattie. No one. She stalked back to her own hut. The outside temperature, in the sun, was nearly a hundred degrees Fahrenheit. Mattie was probably thirty degrees warmer than that, and climbing, when Ryan came back.

'Well?' she demanded.

'Very well indeed,' he said. 'My, aren't we— aggressive!'

'I'll aggressive you!' she threatened. 'What happened?'

'At the council?' he teased. 'They voted for change. And would you believe it, the Chief already had the names of three hundred men—one hundred for training, two hundred for guard duty. Just the number I had in mind! They're walking to El Obeid, starting tomorrow. We'll have a special train run out from Kosti to pick them up. And I've got to get Harry going on a training programme, facilities, housing—there are a million things to do if I could only contact the base.'

'Why don't you tell the witch-doctor?' Mattie said disgustedly. 'He knows where the end of the bush tele-graph is!'

'Does he really? Funny you should know something like that!'

'Just something I picked up,' she muttered.

'You know, I feel a little proud of myself,' he mused. 'Coming up here, making these off-the-cuff arrangements, getting the problem off dead centre. It'll look good on my record. Did you know what the Chief said? He *dreamed* the answer. Would you believe that?'

Condemnation, denial, sarcasm—they all sat on the tip of Mattie's tongue. The deal had been hammered out in the women's quarters, every jot of it. The Mattie Latimore who had just left Boston would have blasted him, torn his reputation to shreds, and buried his ego under cool analysis. But the Mattie Latimore who stood in the sun-baked compound in Topari was an entirely different breed of cat. 'Yes,' she said gently, 'you have reason to be proud of yourself.'

'I couldn't have done it without you to back me up,' he continued. 'Some day, you'll have to tell me what *really* went on in the women's compound.'

'Some day,' she promised vaguely. 'Or maybe I'll save it up to tell my granddaughters.'

'The witch doctor and the bush telegraph?' he asked, looking for confirmation. Mattie clasped both hands behind her back and rocked back and forwards on the balls of her feet, and nodded.

'Then start packing,' grinned Ryan. 'If I can get through, I'll have them send up a helicopter. We can ride our oxcart out of town and switch to something more with-it.' Mattie nodded again. And received a kiss on the tip of her nose before he hurried off.

She watched him go, like a fond mother seeing her favourite son off on his first day at school. 'Lord,' she told herself, 'I didn't realise what a tough racket this marriage game is!'

* * *

At the fourth hour the next day, they had rescued their oxen from the crowd. 'Well, not quite,' chuckled Ryan. 'The grey one was so far gone, I'm damned if they didn't eat it during the festival. But the chief provided us a spare.'

'He doesn't look as if he can make it to El Obeid,' Mattie offered judiciously. 'That must be a good distance away?'

'It certainly is,' Ryan agreed. 'But not to worry. You were right about the witch-doctor. He had a whole radio set-up in his dispensary, and I contacted Harry direct. The chopper left early this morning, and should catch up with us about five in the afternoon. And that ends your great adventure, Mattie. You and I, back in civilisation—at least by nightfall tomorrow. What's the first thought that pops into your mind?'

She ducked her head to hide her grin. 'A nice hot shower,' she said primly.

'Boy, you sure know how to puncture a guy's ego,' mourned Ryan. 'Giddap, oxen!'

The oxen, of course, went when they were ready. And directly behind the cart a guard of honour paraded— sixty Masakin Tiwal warriors, their heads adorned with zebra bands sporting tall, waving ostrich feathers, their six-foot spears gleaming in the sun, their oiled bodies glistening as they stamped out a dance rhythm and chanted.

'I feel like Alice in Wonderland,' Mattie whispered to Ryan as she turned around to watch the tail of their procession. 'A queen and her train. I'll never have another.'

'Yes, you will,' he assured her gently. 'On our wedding day.'

She moved over and nestled up to him. 'You do mean all that, Ryan?'

'Every word,' he promised. 'Don't really trust me, do you?'

'It isn't you,' she sighed. 'I just don't have a lot of experience in this man and woman business. I—don't really think I'd trust *anybody*. Don't be angry. I won't believe it until we come *out* of the church after the ceremony!'

'I'm not angry, love. You've come a long way to find your heart. Things will look better when we get back to the United States.'

'I don't think I'll ever see anything like these days,' Mattie said thoughtfully. 'Like you, those eight days to Topari will always be in my memory. How much did you pay for me?'

'We settled on the price, but not the payment,' he answered. 'At the last minute they sprang a new line on me. All this bargaining wasn't about something *I* was supposed to pay. The custom is for *my relatives* to pay the bill.'

'And how did you wriggle out of that one?'

'I swore a solemn oath that I would go back to my cattle empire in Texas and get my uncles to pony up the payment!'

'But how much?' she insisted.

Ryan looked down at her with a tiny grin playing at the corners of his mouth. 'I'll never tell. But I can tell you *one* thing, it was the highest price paid in the Masakin tribes this year!'

'So what?' she teased. 'I'm worth every dollar of it!'

'Cow,' he corrected. 'The payment has to be in cows, not in dollars.'

'Then you'll be right at home at pay-off time,' she laughed. 'I suppose you know a lot about cows?'

'Don't do that to me,' he groaned. 'Do you know why I left Texas?'

'No, why?'

'Because I hate cows,' he rumbled. 'Milk and good steaks, that's what I like about them. Everything else that goes in between those two ends is out of my line. I spent too many years of my youth chasing the east end of a cow—headed west!'

Mattie wanted to ask him something more, but lost the opportunity. An hour out of Topari the procession stopped, the guard offered them one big Masakin cheer, and Meriam and her mother came up to the wagon.

'We bring the thoughts of the Chief Artafi,' the mother said. 'He wishes you many sons, and fine cattle. You will not forget, Latimore woman, when you come home to your own mother?'

'I will not,' Mattie managed through the tears. 'And you, Meriam. You will come to Kosti?'

'No,' the girl said in her so-precise English. 'This is my fifteenth summer. I begin the search for my husband—for the new chief.'

'Choose wisely,' offered Ryan in an uncharacteristically graceful statement. The two Masakin women walked back to the centre of the guard square, there was one more shout from the men, and the two caravans parted company.

'I really feel badly about leaving,' Mattie said as she watched the women disappear. 'She taught me a lot in a short time.'

'You'll probably see Meriam again,' Ryan consoled her. She wiped her eyes and moved an inch or two away, looking for her own private space for just a moment. 'Not Meriam,' she said. 'Her mother.'

They travelled on in companionable silence. The road meandered in front of them, along formerly dry *wadis* now filled with rain run-off, around the base of more hills, out into the savannah grass that stretched northwards to the horizon. Nothing moved in the heated afternoon sky. Trees could be seen at great distances; one here, another there. Only the thorn acacias stood together in thickets, and they needed the least protection. The oxen plodded and nibbled; when the road wandered left, they went right. A limitless plain, such as America's ancestors saw when they moved west in the wagon trains, Mattie thought.

Topari had dwindled into nothing. The horizon advanced, as if it were scenery in a play, and offstage hands were moving it along. Gradually Mattie's eyes grew heavy. She leaned gently, like a falling tower, until her head landed on Ryan's shoulder. He put up a hand to adjust her to the most comfortable position, but it hardly mattered. She was fast asleep.

It might have been the lack of motion, or the sudden stiffening of Ryan's shoulder that awakened her. One eye blinked open, and as soon as she recognised what was happening Mattie straightened up, fully alert, all systems functioning.

'Keep calm,' cautioned Ryan, laying one hand on her arm.

'Yeah, sure,' she muttered, shivering. The oxcart had just come over the crest of a ridge and halted. Directly in front of them was a thoroughly battered British Saracen, an armoured car, with its gun turret staring them in the face. In the open turret stood Ahmed bin Raschid, in all his desert glory. On both sides of the armoured car a dozen soldiers clustered, their ancient rifles all pointed at the oxcart.

Mattie watched, petrified, as the slim Arab clambered out of his war-wagon and strutted over to them. Ryan's hand tightened on her arm. The soldiers were casually closing in on them. She could see the beads of sweat on their black foreheads, noting with surprise that they were individually different from each other, despite their uniformly camouflaged outfits. They ranged from dark black, with tribal scars on their faces, to the light brown of the northern Arab tribes. They moved cautiously, almost as if they feared the pair in the oxcart.

'Miss Latimore,' Ahmed said sarcastically. She could see the pure hatred gleaming in his dark eyes. And the huge pistol that hung at his belt.

'Let me remind you that we operate under contract from Khartoum,' grated Ryan.

'If that is so,' the Arab said silkily, 'Miss Latimore need only show me her travel permit for this district.'

'Is that what this is all about?' Ryan roared in outrage. 'Some petty little travel permit!' Ahmed made a motion with one hand and two of the soldiers climbed into the wagon, seized Ryan's arms, and forced them both out of the cart.

'Ah, but the law is the law,' Ahmed told him. 'I am forced to—detain—Miss Latimore for questioning. You, Mr Quinn, are entitled to proceed about your lawful business.'

'Be damned if I will!' shouted Ryan, struggling against his captors. Two more soldiers vaulted into the cart to assist.

'In that case,' the Arab leader chuckled, 'I am *forced* to arrest you too, Mr Quinn.'

'I can see it breaks your heart,' Ryan snarled. 'When the government hears about this, Raschid, you'll be in a lot of trouble!'

'Then I suppose I must see that they never hear about it,' the Arab commented. 'A pity, isn't it? There are so many—outlaws—in this area. Dangerous men. They kill without purpose. But of course, a beauty such as our Miss Latimore here—I'm sure they would keep her alive for a little time—for entertainment purposes, shall we say?'

'Oh, my God,' Mattie muttered. 'This isn't real, is it? Tell me it isn't real!'

The soldiers pushed them into line as the Saracen led the way northwards. 'Hey!' she shouted. Ahmed looked around at her. 'You can't leave those animals standing there,' she protested. 'Give them a chance. Either turn them around, or unharness them!'

'Ah, the kind heart,' the Arab laughed. 'Be kind to animals. Of course.' He spat a command at one of his black soldiers. The man threw a puzzled glance at Mattie, then ran back. He urged the oxen around, set their noses on the backtrail, and gave them a slap on the rump. The animals, never really concerned about direction, ambled away. The Saracen started forwards again. The soldiers gave Ryan a push in the back to send him on his way, while Mattie stumbled along beside him, boiling with anger.

'Don't let it get you down,' murmured Ryan.

'No, of course not,' she returned bitterly. 'After all, it's only kidnapping, mayhem, rape, murder. What woman wouldn't be thrilled by it all?'

'That's my girl,' he chuckled. 'Now, save your breath. We can't do much of anything until after nightfall.'

'You mean there's some hope?' she gasped.

'There's always hope, love. We're hardly ten or twelve miles away from Topari. It's that armoured car—once we solve *that* problem, it'll be a piece of cake!'

Mattie put her head down and walked, step by aching step, across the plain, her head spinning with plots and schemes. They came to no good end. I suppose I ought to be satisfied, like the heroines in the books, she thought. I'm going to die beside my beloved. Good lord, what a stupid idea!

Two hours of plodding in the hot sun brought them to a small hill in the middle of the plain. Two old baobab trees stretched skyward to offer some shelter. An old truck, as battered as the armoured car, stood in the shade, and cooking fires were lit. They were urged up the incline by the soldiers behind them, urged into the shelter of a grimy canvas tent, and pushed down on to the dirt floor. Two of the men tied them loosely to a rope tether and attached the other end to one of the tent-poles. Then they took up guard positions at the tent-flap.

An hour later, as twilight fell, Ahmed bin Raschid swaggered into their prison tent. 'An excellent meal,' he commented. He was using a gold toothpick on his perfect teeth.

'You can't get away with this,' Ryan said coolly.

'I don't see why not,' the Arab said pleasantly. 'We are having a little trouble setting up our radio. After that, I shall offer Miss Latimore a chance to buy you some supper—and maybe even extend your lives.' He bent down and ran a hand through Mattie's blonde hair. 'Strange, what an attraction blondes are for men of my race,' he mused. 'I must have patience. I'm sure it will increase my pleasure when I sample the rest of her. You do like me a little, don't you, my dear?'

Arabic was her only answer. It had the better selection of words, the most tasty phrases. 'As I like a pig,' she told him in that graceful, flowing language. 'A pig, greased in slime. Your mother was undoubtedly a camel driver, your father an Israeli whore-master, and all your sisters have dung between their toes!'

'*Ya bint*,' he muttered wrathfully. 'You will learn better!' His hand slammed against her cheek, knocking her over into Ryan's lap.

'Easy,' Ryan whispered as Ahmed stalked out of the tent. 'Play it cool. Look at the guard.'

In the darkness, it was almost impossible for Mattie to see anything in particular, until one of the soldiers stuck his head inside the tent, holding a flare. Across his forehead, the tribal cicatrices glared at her. 'Good heavens,' she muttered. 'Masakin!'

'It's a polyglot army,' Ryan hissed. 'Just sit quietly. When I give you the word, run like hell for the armoured car!'

'But I don't understand,' she moaned.

'We're in the middle of an empty plain,' he explained in a whisper. 'If *they* have the car, they can track us down in a minute. If *we* have the car, they can't do a thing! Got it?'

Mattie nodded, trying to look like a girl who not only understood, but had faith in any escape plan. Neither was true, but for some reason she wanted him to have confidence in her. Ryan watched her for a moment, and then began speaking in a soft, compelling voice. It was the Nuban language. She even recognised a word here and there. The soldier on guard moved closer, staring, as if trying to read his lips. Ryan repeated what he had said twice, the soldier's mouth fell open in surprise, and he transferred his stare to her.

'My accent isn't too good,' Ryan told her in English. 'Now, don't be frightened, and for the love of God, don't scream!'

'N-no,' she stammered, already half out of her wits. The soldier was a young man, full of his warrior strength. He came around Ryan and squatted down beside her. Mattie sat up, shivering. The soldier laid his rifle down on the ground, and one of his hands came to the buttons of her blouse. Good lord in heaven! she thought to

herself. Don't scream? Instead of Ahmed, I get this—
soldier? Ryan's bargained me off for an escape plan?

The warrior fumbled with the unfamiliar buttons, then
growled deep in his throat. One of his muscular hands
tangled in the collar of her blouse, and with one massive
heave he tore it away. But it wasn't rape he had in mind.
He moved behind her, uncovered her left shoulder, and
sat back on his haunches. She could hear the hiss of his
breath, expelled in anger. He said something to Ryan,
repeating it three times. Then he softly called the other
guard into the tent, brushing aside the torn strap of her
camisole so that both could peer. Mattie looked fear-
fully over her shoulder. They held the flare close—so
close she could feel the warmth of the flame—as they
studied the tattoo markings embedded in her skin.

Without warning, they doused the flare, leaving the
tent in darkness. A few more words were exchanged.
One of them slipped quietly out of the tent and disappeared into the darkness. It was all more than Mattie
could handle. She sat up straight in the darkness, tears
falling from her eyes, her throat choked up with pain.
When Ryan moved over beside her and his arm came
around her shoulders she crumpled, falling into his chest,
seeking the comfort that only touch could bring. For a
moment she lay there sobbing, and then her brain came
back on line. His arm around my shoulders? With his
hands tied? She sat up again, just as another hand
fumbled with her own bindings, and the pressure of the
ropes was gone.

'Masakin,' he told her in a whisper. 'They recognise
your tribal markings. See—you're making this whole
thing easy!'

It *was* easy. The Saracen was parked a few paces from
their tent, and all the soldiers were gathered around the
cooking fires, eating. They crawled the distance, keeping

off the skyline. Ryan pushed Mattie up the turret, and she tumbled into the armour-protected well of the car. He followed close behind, and the Masakin guard behind him closed the turret lid and locked it.

'But the other guard?' she whispered.

'We're only a few miles from Topari,' he reminded her. 'He's gone for help. Running all the way, something ought to happen by daybreak tomorrow.'

'Daybreak?' she gasped. But why don't we just—drive away?'

'Because your friend Ahmed is a little too wily,' Ryan retorted. 'He's not afraid of us, but of his own soldiers. He has the fuel drained out of the tanks of the vehicles every night!'

'And we just *sit* here?' Now that they were out of that tent, her Latimore anger was riding at full steam. 'I'm sure there's a *little* fuel in those tanks. And that's a—a machine-gun right there!'

His hands made a casual inspection in the dark. 'With no ammunition,' he reported. 'But there *is* a little fuel left in the system!'

'And what are we going to do?'

'Sit tight. When they discover we're missing, we're going to drive this thing right over that field table over there, and smash the hell out of his radio.'

'Well, I'm sure that will make him sorry,' Mattie said sarcastically.

'You bet it will,' he returned in the same vein. 'He won't be able to call for help. Now, for God's sake, will you please sit down?'

'Thank you, Mr Quinn,' she answered in a very small voice.

CHAPTER TEN

EASTBORO was a tiny New England village, located south of Boston. It contained a single shopping street three blocks long and an old wooden church, painted white, with its graveyard just behind it. The hand of early summer lay gently on the land, and nature perfumed the air. One block away from the church the Latimore house stood, crenellated neo-Baroque, crowned by towers and bay windows, and a broad, screened veranda. Mattie shared the swinging lounge with her tiny mother. Her seventeen-year-old sister Faith sat on the top stair. Fourteen-year-old Hope balanced precariously on the porch rail, and twelve-year-old Michael, sturdy and solid like his father, and already inches taller than his mother, stood with hands in pockets, doubting.

'And then what happened, Mattie?' he prodded.

Mattie leaned forward in her eagerness to make it all sound like adventure, even though her heart was breaking. Mary-Kate knew—she was a mother for all seasons, and even though her strawberry hair sparkled with white, and her slim figure was just the slightest bit plumper than it once had been, Mary-Kate kept her finger on the pulse of youth.

'Well,' Mattie said, 'they didn't find out we'd escaped from the tent until just before dawn. They made an awful lot of noise, stumbling around in the dark, and that's when Ryan——' her voice caught on a tear, then broke free '—Ryan started up the engine of the armoured car and turned on the headlights. All the soldiers shouted, and a couple of them shot at us, but the bullets bounced off. Gee, that sounded funny! And then Ryan just put it in gear and ran right over that radio table and smashed everything to bits.'

'And then you killed all the bad guys?' probed Michael.

'Not exactly,' Mattie laughed. 'We just managed to move as far as the radio table, and we ran out of fuel. So Ryan told us to sit tight, and we did. The soldiers ran around like a pack of ants, climbed all over the armoured car, but they couldn't get in, you know.'

'And of course you couldn't get out,' Faith interjected. 'Crazy, the pair of you! You deserved each other.'

'Now, missy,' her mother said quietly, 'it's Mattie's story. Go ahead, dear.'

'Well, there isn't much left to tell,' Mattie sighed. 'We couldn't get out, and they couldn't get in, and then the sun came up. And there they were! Wow, we were all astonished! Especially Ahmed bin Raschid.'

'There who were?' Hope asked.

'Five hundred Masakin warriors!' Mattie remembered that surprise with glee. 'They came up during the night and formed a circle completely around the hill. And there they stood, with those eight-foot spears in their hands, blocking all the roads in every direction!'

'Tell again how tall they was,' Michael insisted.

'Big,' laughed Mattie. 'Masakin Tiwal they were—all over six foot six, and with those big plumes in their hair. They looked like five hundred Boston Celtics who'd forgotten their basketballs!'

'Nobody's as big as Larry Bird,' sceptical Michael commented.

'Well, these were,' Mattie said severely. 'Bigger. Do you want to hear this story or not?'

'Go ahead,' Hope insisted. 'What does *he* know?'

'Well, anyway, Ahmed ordered his soldiers to shoot at the warriors, but they were too smart for that. They knew they might get in one shot, perhaps two, and then the warriors would be all over them. So they laid down their guns and surrendered. Ahmed was so mad, he pulled out his revolver and was about to shoot, when Ryan jumped out of the armoured car and landed right on top of him. And he beat him up most terribly! And that's about the end of the story. The Masakin took Ahmed away with them and he—disappeared. And the helicopter arrived and carried Mr Quinn and me back to the Kosti camp, and that's all.'

Mary-Kate checked her wrist-watch. 'And now it's time for the three of you to get over to the farm,' she announced. 'You all promised Uncle Henry you'd come and help with the chickens tonight.'

'I don't want to help with any chickens,' snapped Hope. 'Chickens—yuck!'

'That's enough, missy,' her mother said firmly. The girl swallowed her rebellion immediately.

'I'll drive us over,' said Faith, unfolding gracefully from the stairs.

'Not me,' Michael announced. 'I ain't gonna risk my life with *you* driving!'

'How's about risking a punch in the mouth?' his sister offered, and they went down the stairs, still arguing pleasantly, as siblings do.

'And now,' said Mary-Kate, 'tell me the *rest* of the story.'

'Oh, Ma!' Mattie responded. 'That's—all there is.'

'Of course,' her mother returned. 'I sent a lovely vibrant young lady out to Africa, and she comes home six weeks later, worn to the bone, twenty pounds underweight, and shoulders bent under the weight of the world.' She was inches shorter than her daughter, but the girl came to her arms just the same.

'We all have bad times, Mattie. When little John was born—and died so quickly—I thought my heart would break. But I had your father, and all of you, and duties that called, and I went back to work. It helped. But mostly it was your father's big shoulder for me to cry on. Come on now, girl.'

'Well——' Mattie stopped to dab at a tiny tear forming in one eye. 'He said he loved me. We were going to be married. Only the minute we got back to camp, he disappeared into his wife's quarters——'

'Oh, my! You knew he was married?'

'Yes,' Mattie sighed. 'I mean—no. They were divorced, but she warned me—said they were bound together by chains forged in hell, and he could never break free! I'd forgotten on the trip, but——'

'There now, child, let it all out,' soothed Mary-Kate.

'We were all so terribly busy for the next few days—making plans for the school, a campsite, food—all that. And then a week after we got back I suddenly realised I hadn't seen him in three days. I cornered Harry Crampton at the office, and he—he said he thought Ryan had *told* me. That Ryan and Virginia had left three days before, flying out to Texas!'

'And he left you no word?'

'Nothing. For a week, I sat around like a leaky radiator, crying, but there was just—no word. So I finally said to hell with him, and I came home!'

Her mother made soft, soothing noises, stroking the girl's golden hair.

'Ma?'

'Yes, love?'

'Are men all like that?'

'Not *good* men, love. Put it all behind you. Go back to work, keep yourself busy, and let time do its work.'

There followed a week when the family walked around on tiptoe, respecting Mattie's privacy while itching for information. Even her father could think of little to do to help his aching daughter. Only Mary-Kate contained in her enough of the soothing balm to make the hurt subside—for a time.

And Michael, who knew only that some man had made Mattie cry, offered his own solution. 'Just tell me where he lives,' he said at the dinner table one night, 'and I'll go pound his head for him.'

'Amen,' his father commented. 'I'd go myself, but I'm getting a little long in the tooth.'

'See your dentist twice a year,' chanted Hope, to be instantly shushed by the family.

The nights were the worst time. Tired or fresh, everywhere Mattie turned the night reflected the magic time at Topari. She could see their slow progression behind the oxen as the miles followed each other in solemn succession. She could recall each movement, each second, from the silly day when the Land Rover was struck by lightning to that last night on the road, when she had finally realised she loved Ryan Quinn.

And so Mattie Latimore cried her grief away, drew sustenance from the love that surrounded her, and a week after she came home from Africa she drove her little Triumph up the highway to Boston, and went back to work.

'Try this one,' her father suggested. 'Belfair. They want a new town hall. Something that doesn't look like the Tower of London, or a packet of Wheaties, and can be had for something under a hundred thousand dollars.'

'I'll give it a look,' she prómised, 'but one of those parameters has to stretch. We could hardly design and build a doghouse in that price range!' She took the package of requirements and walked back to her own office, whistling. Everyone around her took it for happiness, for a return to normality, but her father knew better. 'Whistling past the graveyard,' Mary-Kate always said.

Mattie wondered why her father never questioned her. As close as she was to her parents, she had never realised that everything Mary-Kate knew, Bruce knew. And vice versa. It was the way they lived, that pair. As close to being one person as was physically possible.

Mattie looked over the outlines from Belfair, took a run out to the site one cloudy day, and sat back to think. Which was the proper way to begin any design problem. But Africa still bothered her, so on occasion she dropped off at the Sudanese project office to check up.

Andy Frame was the project engineer. One of the new generation in the Latimore Corporation, he was a young and brash Californian, who ruled his little project with an iron fist. And kept a weather eye out for the boss's daughter. Not Mattie—she was too much her own woman. Faith was the girl he watched. Lean, beautiful Faith, who wanted to be a lawyer.

'Well, we have a few updates,' he told Mattie cautiously. 'The railroad is running, all the way from Kosti to Darfur province. Twelve apprentice locomotive engineers have made the round trip. On two occasions, representatives from the Dinka tribe were induced not to destroy culverts on the line——'

'And what a mouthful that must cover!' laughed Mattie.

'What?'

'What they're saying is that the rebels made two raids on the rail line and Masakin warriors turned them away!'

'God, that's not civilised,' Andy Frame said squeamishly.

'No, it really isn't,' Mattie agreed, judging the man, and finding him not up to the Latimore standards. She broached the subject to her father the next day at lunch in the cafeteria.

'I know,' he told her. 'But there's a place for everybody, Mattie. I'm still trying to find the right place for young Mr Frame. As far as the Sudan project is concerned, Quinn's solution seems ideal. The trains are running, the government is happy, the school project is going like wildfire. But——'

'But?'

'Two *buts*,' he laughed, reaching for the pie à la mode.

'Whoa!' said Mattie, tapping on his big wrist. 'Ma said—— '

'Now don't you go giving me orders, young lady. I'm old enough to be your father!'

'Yes, sir,' she grinned. 'Only Ma said if I caught you going off your diet I was to tell her immediately. So I guess I'll have to put another long-distance telephone call on my expense account.'

'How about that!' he groaned. 'Spies in my own family! I'm probably the most henpecked man in the state!'

'You and Michael,' she teased. 'Now, about the *buts*?'

He pulled his hand sheepishly back from the dessert tray. 'Ah yes, the buts. Well, the first one. What you two did in the back country was to start the Masakin on a great change, out of the primitive into the modern. I'm not sure that was a wise thing to do. They seemed to have been happy in their backward way.'

'I'm not too sure myself,' Mattie confessed. 'But look at the alternatives. They were falling behind, and their neighbours were pressing on their little frontiers. So was the central government. If they had done nothing, their culture would have disappeared, and them with it. There was no place left to which they might have migrated. Half a million people can't just up and move—not these days. They're an immensely intelligent people; by moving out of the Stone Age they may have posed problems for themselves, but then again, they might be an important part of the glue needed to stick the Sudan together as a nation. And what was the other *but*?'

'The other but is more important, love.' He leaned across the table and took his daughter's hand. 'Ryan Quinn is an outstanding man. He sent in notice that he wouldn't be renewing his contract with us. Counting leave time, he's been unemployed since last Monday.'

Mattie did her best to shrug it off, to appear not to be interested at all in the fate of Ryan Quinn. She said as much.

'Come on now,' her father coaxed. 'I know better than that.'

'Well, I just don't care about him, or what he does, or where he is,' she snapped, then stopped talking to look up tearfully up at her father. 'Where is he?' Her voice was on the edge of breaking.

'Back in the United States,' he returned casually. 'Not in Texas. I really don't know exactly.'

'Well, I don't care,' she averred strongly. 'He could be in—in—Timbuktu, for all I care. I think I'll take the afternoon off. I have some——' I have some crying to do, she told herself, and then I'm going to put him out of my mind and never think of him again. Never!

'You have some what?' her father prompted. Mattie jumped, having almost forgotten he was there.

'I have some—shopping to do,' she said firmly. 'All my clothes are out of date or out of the country.'

'Good idea,' her father chuckled. 'Eat a little. Put on a few pounds, give some man a thrill.'

'Hah, men!' she snorted, and left him to pay the bill.

Mattie was home by four o'clock, upstairs in her own little suite, trying to be some help. Her sister Hope was up to her neck in algebra, and going down for the third time.

'I don't see how anyone who can play the violin so well would have trouble with simple algebra,' Mattie exclaimed, and proceeded to put the situation to rights.

'Well, the violin is real,' her sister grumbled. 'I hate this theoretical stuff. I need something I can put my hands on!'

There was a large rumble of motors outside the window, and Hope wandered over to look. 'Just a couple of big trucks,' she reported back. 'Now, if I take this equation, I—I forgot already.'

'The product of the means is equal to the product of the extremes,' chanted Mattie. 'Say it fifty times.'

'Can't,' giggled Hope. 'I have a date with Rimsky-Korsakov.'

There was more noise outside. Animal noises. Clatter. And a call from downstairs. Sister Faith, standing on the second-floor landing, called at the top of the voice, 'Mattie!'

Mattie put her pencils carefully away. 'No rest for the wicked,' her little sister teased from behind her.

'It looks that way,' Mattie returned as she walked out of the room into the hall. 'What is it, Faith? And don't yell at me like a fishwife!'

'Never mind the fish,' her sister called up excitedly. 'There's someone here. Ma wants you right away in the parlour! Right away, Mattie!'

'OK, I'm coming,' Mattie chuckled. Faith was a girl of great excitements. When she liked something she glowed; anything else was classed as 'the pits', and brought on depression and pimples. 'What's all the excitement?'

'I don't know,' Faith replied as they passed each other. 'But it *has* to be important to be in the parlour!'

And that's true, Mattie told herself, hurrying just a little faster. Her mother was not *old*, but she was of Old New England stock. The parlour was a room closed off from normal living, its double doors kept closed, reserved for funerals, weddings, and visits from the parish pastor. So, automatically, anything assigned to the parlour was of importance.

The noise outside was rising from 'disturbance' to 'havoc' proportions, but the lace curtains on the windows in front left Mattie no view as she hurried down the ground-floor corridor and opened the door into the parlour.

'Mathilda,' her mother said. It wasn't her 'motherly' voice, filled with tailings of laughter, but rather her professional 'judge's' voice—like, 'bring the guilty rascal in and we'll give him a fair trial!' And nobody called Mattie Mathilda—except for her grandmother in Newport, whom she hated with a passion. She turned around, adjusting her eyes to the lesser light of the parlour.

Her mother was sitting upright and stern on the couch. Across from her, sunk into one of the upholstered chairs built for her father, was—Ryan Quinn!

Mattie froze. Every muscle in her being refused to move——

'Mathilda,' her mother said, 'this gentleman feels that you have breached a contract with him, and he's come to demand a settlement.'

'He what?' she stammered, unable to keep her eyes off his stern, uncompromising face. 'What contract?'

'Mr Quinn?'

He faced Mary-Kate. 'In the month of June,' he re-cited, as if he were before the bench, 'she agreed to mar-riage with me. In support of that contract I made a true and legal bargain with certain representatives of the Masakin tribe, in the absence of her legal parents, and agreed to a proper purchase price for you as my bride.'

'But—but——' Mattie stammered. 'I——'

'Do you deny that you were, at that time, a member of the Masakin tribe, under the authority of Chief Artafi?'

'No—I——'

'Do you question the right of the tribal Chief to ap-point a legitimate representative to bargain for you?'

'I—no, I——'

'Do you deny that I met with that representative and made a bargain for your purchase?'

'I—I don't know,' she flamed. 'They wouldn't let me come near to find out. Besides, you didn't *pay* the bride-price, you just *agreed* to the price.'

'It would seem that that's what Mr Quinn has come to do,' Mary-Kate interrupted. The little laugh-devils were back in her voice. 'Mr Quinn tells me he's travelled all this distance——'

'Because you ran out on me,' Ryan interrupted. 'I went all the way back to Kosti to get you and you'd disappeared! What kind of a bargain is that?'

Mattie refused to look at him any longer. It did strange things to her stomach, and she wanted no more disadvantages. So instead she stared at her mother. 'Ask him about his wife—about Virginia,' she muttered.

'Mr Quinn?'

'She's not my wife!' he thundered. 'We were legally divorced six years ago.'

'But—but you left me in Kosti, and—I thought—she said——'

'Mrs Latimore, may I explain this thing to you?' Ryan cut in. 'It's almost impossible for me to explain anything to your daughter.'

'If you like, Mr Quinn. Please sit down again. Can I get you some refreshment?'

'No, I—I couldn't eat a bite. Just looking at this—at your daughter infuriates me!'

'Yes, I can see it does,' agreed Mary-Kate. 'Mattie, please sit down. I don't want you hovering over me like a hundred-and-twenty-pound butterfly. Now, Mr Quinn?'

'Yes.' He cleared his throat. 'My *former* wife was in the Kosti camp. When Mattie and I escaped from Ahmed, we took a helicopter back there, and I went immediately to hunt Virginia out of her hiding-place. It was she who had told Ahmed where to find us. She intercepted our radio call about the helicopter, and immediately passed the information on!'

'I didn't know that,' Mattie interrupted indignantly. 'She could have had us killed!'

'Shut up,' Ryan rumbled at her. 'It's my turn to talk.' He turned back to her mother. 'So you see, Mrs

Latimore, I was a little upset about all this, and I figured your *very mature* daughter would understand, and spare me——'

'You don't have to be so sarcastic!' Mattie shouted at him. 'How the hell was I——'

'Now, missy,' her mother interrupted. 'Bad language can never make a good situation.' Mattie blushed and sank back in her chair. 'Go on, Mr Quinn.'

'Thank you, ma'am.' Listen to him put on the Texas drawl! Mattie told herself hysterically. He thinks he can bamboozle my mother the way he did me! Her heart skipped a painful beat at the thought.

'So,' Ryan continued, 'I finally tracked my *former* wife down, hiding in one of the camp buildings, and she promptly collapsed in what the doctor said was a complete breakdown, which would do her permanent damage if we didn't get her to a Stateside hospital. So I left instructions with Jensen, and——'

'Jensen?' Mattie screeched. 'That insignificant little kid, Jensen?'

'That's the one,' snapped Ryan. 'You were so damn busy with the training programme out in the railroad yards that I couldn't get an appointment with you!'

'Oh, my,' Mattie said softly, and collapsed back into her chair again. It was true. For a few days she had shut herself off from everything in order to get the programme running. And poor little Jensen——

'Jensen,' she said pleadingly. 'He came down with dengue fever. We had to evacuate him.'

'Oh——!' muttered Ryan. 'Don't tell me you didn't get my message?'

'No, I won't tell you, but I didn't even know you were gone until—why did you go?'

'I told you,' he said. 'I mean, I explained it to your mother. I had to get Virginia out of there in a hurry. Somebody had to accompany her. I was the only one who knew anything about her, so I was elected. She's down in the Texas Medical Center now. They figure that with two or three years' careful treatment she may snap out of it.'

'Oh, God,' moaned Mattie. 'I was so damn jealous! I almost ate my fingers to the bone with worrying about you!'

'And so that's my case, Mrs Latimore,' said Ryan. 'We have a valid contract, your daughter and I. Outside I have the agreed bride-price. Thirty-two cows, four of them already pregnant. One bullock. Four goats. Sixteen chickens.'

'Well!' Mary-Kate got up from her couch, fluttering. 'Mattie?'

'Oh, God, what a fool I've been,' groaned Mattie. 'Ryan?'

He made no answer. Instead, he stood up, faced her, and opened his arms. She ran across the space that separated them and threw herself into the warm comfort. His head came down on hers, isolating her from the rest of the world, sweeping her away from here and now to that loving place in his heart. Mary-Kate rubbed a tear out of her own eye and walked towards the door.

'My husband is the only one who can acknowledge payment,' she called to the pair of them. Neither seemed to have heard. From the front door she heard a roar of anger.

'Who the hell is responsible for this mess?' Bruce Latimore had arrived home right on cue. Smiling, Mary-Kate went out into the hall, partially closing the double doors of the parlour behind her.

'Who owns all those—animals out there?' Bruce shouted.

It had no effect on Mary-Kate. After twenty years of marriage, she had become accustomed to his roars. 'You do,' she said, snuggling up against him.

'Me?' He looked down at her suspiciously.

'You,' she repeated quietly. He was boasting a slight paunch, this wonderful man of hers, and his forehead was perhaps an inch or two higher than it once had been, and sprinkled with salt, but she loved him all the same.

'I suppose you're going to tell me about it?' he asked.

'There's a man in the parlour kissing your daughter Mathilda,' she explained, trying hard not to laugh. 'It would appear that while they were in Africa he bought her.'

'He bought my daughter?'

'Dad!' shouted Michael, racing in through the back door. 'Some guy's in the parlour making out with Mattie!'

'Is he really?' Bruce Latimore too had learned something in twenty years. Although living with Mary-Kate was like a permanent trip over breaking ice, it was also a great deal of fun.

'Thirty-two cows, four already pregnant,' Mary-Kate counted off her fingers. 'Four goats. One bullock. And I forget how many chickens. Her bride-price.'

'I take it that they're——'

'In the parlour.' His little wife straightened his tie. He shrugged his shoulders and walked into the room. Ryan Quinn jumped up hastily, and Mattie, who had been sitting in his lap, barely managed to avoid being dumped on the floor. She ducked behind Ryan, fumbling to re-do a couple of buttons.

'I hear you plan to marry my daughter?' Bruce said in his most impressive executive voice.

'I believe I do,' replied Ryan, equally assured.

'And these—er—animals on my lawn? They're the agreed price?'

'To the chicken,' the young man in front of him responded.

'In that case,' said Bruce, 'I accept your offer. Got two *more* daughters I have to marry off, you know.' He turned to leave, then had an afterthought. 'And by the way, Quinn, those animals are legally mine as of this moment, but all that manure on my new lawn—that's still yours. See to it!' He stalked out of the room, a big smile on his face. It matched the grins on the two faces behind in the parlour as Ryan swung Mattie back into his arms. In the distance they could hear the family talking.

'Michael,' Mary-Kate scolded. 'Get away from that parlour door! You all come and have your supper before it gets cold!'

'What's for supper, Ma?' asked Hope.

'Cold cuts,' she told her.

'Good God,' Ryan muttered in Mattie's ear. 'Are they all nuts?'

'Everyone but me,' she murmured. 'You're lucky you caught the right one!'

He kissed her again, very satisfactorily. Or so she judged. The pair of them fell back into the overstuffed chair, laughing, and his hands wandered.

'Damn buttons,' he growled. 'Every time I get them undone something happens. Another one of your Calvinist problems?'

'Not me,' she smiled. 'From here on in you're on your own, buster!'

'We have to have a wedding, Mattie!'

'Don't worry, ' she whispered, 'Ma will take care of that.'

'So I'd better get me a hotel room?'

'In Eastboro? You must be kidding! No hotels; no motels.'

'So what the hell do I do until the wedding?'

'You're doing fine just where you are,' she said. 'But my sister Rebecca lives in Middleboro——'

'That's nice. How do you unfasten this thing?'

'A clip at the back,' she sighed, then squeaked as Ryan found the answer and marched two fingers up to the peak of her breast. The silence was broken only by distant mumbling from the family at dinner, and a deep moan from Mattie.

'I don't think I can wait around too long,' he said, his voice laden with tension.

'Me neither,' she sighed. 'My sister Rebecca. She owns a farmhouse just across town. It's empty except for weekends.'

'So?'

'So today is Monday,' Mattie gasped. 'You could stay at the farmhouse, but then you'd need somebody to take care of you—food and laundry and—things, and I could do that until Ma gets the wedding set, and——'

'I like the sound of that—*and things*,' Ryan told her. 'When can we leave?'

There was a feeling of desperation in Mattie's voice as his fingers wandered on. 'Right now,' she gasped. 'I can't wait—— God, Ryan, I love you!'

'And I love you,' he muttered, frustrated. He picked her up, all dishevelled, and stalked out of the house. The front door slammed behind them.

Back in the dining-room, Bruce Latimore shook his head as he heard the door close. His wife gave him a warning glance and kicked his ankle.

'Times have changed,' Mary-Kate hissed at him.

'Yeah,' Bruce said mournfully, 'but how about my lawn?'

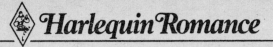
Harlequin Romance

Coming Next Month

2971 REMEMBER, IN JAMAICA Katherine Arthur
For three years Claire has battled with her boss over his violent temper, impossible dreams and insane schedules. Suddenly, once she agrees to the working trip in Jamaica, Terrill changes into a pussycat. Claire can't help feeling suspicious.

2972 NO LOVE IN RETURN Elizabeth Barnes
The only reason Eve has worked as a model is to pay for her brother's education. To the imperious Jackson Sinclair, however, *model* is synonymous with *gold digger*. And there seems to be no way to persuade him he's wrong.

2973 SNOWFIRE Dana James
Beth can't pass up the chance to be official photographer on an Iceland expedition, though she's stunned to find her estranged husband, Dr. Allan Bryce, as leader. Even more shocking is the realization that Allan thinks he was the injured party!

2974 SYMPATHETIC STRANGERS Annabel Murray
Recently widowed Sandra begins to build a new life for herself and her young twins by helping friends of her mother's in Kent. Yet when lord of the manor Griff Faversham pursues her, she refuses to consider marriage to another wealthy man.

2975 BED, BREAKFAST & BEDLAM Marcella Thompson
In helping Bea McNair establish an Ozark Mountain retreat for Bea's ailing friends, Janet dismisses Lucas McNair's plan to move his mother to a Little Rock retirement home. There's no dismissing Lucas, though, when he descends upon her like a wrathful God.

2976 MOWANA MAGIC Margaret Way
Ally can't deny the attraction between herself and the powerful Kiall Lancaster, despite his mistrust of her. Common sense tells her to leave. But first she determines to straighten out Kiall's chauvinistic attitude. Not an easy task!

Available in April wherever paperback books are sold, or through Harlequin Reader Service:

In the U.S.
901 Fuhrmann Blvd.
P.O. Box 1397
Buffalo, N.Y. 14240-1397

In Canada
P.O. Box 603
Fort Erie, Ontario
L2A 5X3

Harlequin Regency Romance™

Romance the way it was *always* meant to be!

The time is 1811, when a Regent Prince rules the empire. The place is London, the glittering capital where rakish dukes and dazzling debutantes scheme and flirt in a dangerously exciting game. Where marriage is the passport to wealth and power, yet every girl hopes secretly for love....

Welcome to Harlequin Regency Romance where reading is an adventure and romance is *not* just a thing of the past! Two delightful books a month, beginning May '89.

Available wherever Harlequin Books are sold.

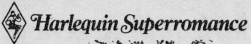

COMING IN MARCH FROM

◆ *Harlequin*
  Superromance

**Book Two of the
Merriman County Trilogy
AFTER ALL THESE YEARS
the sizzle of Eve Gladstone's
One Hot Summer continues!**

Sarah Crewes is at it again, throwing Merriman County
into a tailspin with her archival diggings. In *One Hot
Summer* (September 1988) she discovered that the town
of Ramsey Falls was celebrating its tricentennial one
year too early.

Now she's found that Riveredge, the Creweses'
ancestral home and property, does not rightfully belong
to her family. Worse, the legitimate heir to Riveredge
may be none other than the disquieting Australian,
Tyler Lassiter.

Sarah's not sure why Tyler's in town, but she suspects
he is out to right some old wrongs—and some new
ones!

The unforgettable characters of *One Hot Summer* and
After All These Years will continue to delight you in
book three of the trilogy. Watch for *Wouldn't It Be
Lovely* in November 1989.

Have You Ever Wondered If You Could Write A Harlequin Novel?

Here's great news—Harlequin is offering a series of cassette tapes to help you do just that. Written by Harlequin editors, these tapes give practical advice on how to make your characters—and your story—come alive. There's a tape for each contemporary romance series Harlequin publishes.

Mail order only

All sales final
